A book of poetry wrapped in a novel…

Enjoy

Chapter One
Moving On

"Lock the door on the way out," Jess said as she turned on her side and pulled the blanket over her shoulder.

Marcus, Marquis, Mar-*something*! Whatever his name was, he was exactly what she needed after finding out the love of her life had cheated. Again.

Well, "love of her life" might've been a bit strong. They'd only been together for eight months, but this was the third time she'd caught him cheating.

Jess was frustrated and hurt. She thought he'd be different. When Erick walked into her family's African Spirituality shop, Jess felt him. As he approached to ask her advice on a few crystals he was debating purchasing, her heart sped up. They looked at each other and she felt like she was in a movie. Their frequencies seemed to align as they shared a smile.

They exchanged phone numbers, and their romance quickly began. Days of laughter and nights of passion consumed her entire world until she got her first "Coming to you as a woman" text message.

Apparently, Erick wasn't entirely done with his relationship with Tia, the woman he'd been seeing before the day he walked into Jess's shop. Tia went through Erick's phone and found text messages between him and Jess. Erick was lying next to Jess when she received the message. She listened as he explained that his ex was jealous and nothing was happening between them. He told Jess it was a recent breakup, but Tia couldn't let the relationship go.

Against every red flag that waved in front of her eyes and every alarm bell that rang in her head, Jess decided she would believe him. Clearly that was a mistake because less than two months later she caught him cheating again.

This time with a server at a restaurant downtown they'd visited. Though the server's name escaped her, she remembered her energy. Jess's intuition was confirmed when she went through Erick's phone while he was in the shower.

Erick thought he was slick when he'd given her his passcode after the first suspected indiscretion. Jess allowed him to believe she would never use it, that her security and trust in him was in knowing he allowed her to have it. As she unlocked his phone and found pictures and text messages, she couldn't help shaking her head at how naïve he was to believe she'd never check. She only needed a reason to use his passcode and his behavior the last time they visited the restaurant, and the side-eyes she'd received from their server, was more than enough. Jess even chuckled when she saw the number saved under the restaurant's name. How dumb did he think she was?

Jess actually walked away that time. For a week. When he showed up at her door with flowers and an actual tear-filled apology, she decided to give him one more chance. Things seemed incredible until three days ago when the ex-girlfriend, yup Tia, came around for a repeat appearance.

Jess was done. Finished! She believed the first time the shame was on him. The second time she accepted the shame for herself. However, the third time...well, she would be a complete fool to allow it to continue. It was painfully obvious he had no intention of ever changing. Their love wasn't enough. The laughter wasn't enough. Their shared energy wasn't enough. He needed more, and she decided she would not stick around to find out what that was. If he wanted her to know he would have told her on his own. Even through this lapse of judgment she knew her worth. She was too good for this and had too much pride to allow any other woman to continue to believe she had one up on her.

The first time she got the text message, she ignored it, but the last time she answered with a simple response: *You got it sis...enjoy.* With that, she screenshot the short conversation, sent it to Erick, then blocked them both.

Getting over him wouldn't be too hard; she knew she would be fine, but the frustration of having gone through it kept her up at night. Last night she'd decided to occupy her mind, so she went to a bar downtown. Even though Jess was known to be a free spirit, she wasn't in the habit of bringing home strange men. Any man she encountered on occasion would never be allowed into her personal space, but throwing caution to the wind, she brought home Mar- what was his name?

Shaking her head in frustration that she couldn't remember the name of the man with the perfectly sculpted body, amazing cologne, and the ability to make her completely forget anything or anyone else existed, she picked up her phone.

"I know you're in Jamaica living your best life, but girl!" Jess said into the screen as she looked at her beautiful friend Mahogany.

Mahogany smiled as the sun shone in the background allowing her melanin to glisten on the screen.

"What did you do?" Mahogany asked.

"Marvin!" Jess paused, "Malik," she paused again, "Well whatever his name is...he was fine and slang that thang like-"

"Jess!"

"Huh?"

"Slow down," Mahogany said, laughing.

Jess exhaled. She knew she tended to start a story right in the middle, which drove her friends crazy...in the most endearing way possible.

"My bad," she said with a laugh.

Mahogany squinted her eyes, "Now who is this guy and where is Erick?"

"He cheated again."

"Awe, I'm sorry, love."

"Honestly, it's okay," Jess responded quickly, "I mean I'm not okay with it all, but it is what it is."

Mahogany exhaled and Jess took in her best friend's unspoken words of comfort.

"So Mr. M. was a rebound," it was more of a statement from Mahogany than a question.

"Yup," Jess responded, "A great distraction."

"When I get back we'll have some wine and talk," Mahogany said with the compassion Jess needed.

"Most definitely," Jess paused and cleared her mind from her own issues, "Tell me you found a fine Jamaican man to rub coconut oil on your booty!" Jess said with a huge grin.

The two friends continued their conversation as Jess allowed herself to live vicariously through the adventures of Mahogany's quest to find her artistic muse on the island of Jamaica.

*****

As the sun began to set, Jess felt her urge to write grow in her belly. Where Mahogany's solace came from painting, poetry had always been Jess's escape, her therapy. The way words flowed through her fingertips and out through the ink that landed on blank pages was like a lyrical mural. Her gift was known throughout the city, and her presence was always welcome at Verse One, the local open mic. So as she finished her most recent piece, she dressed and headed out the door.

As she walked through the door of Verse One she was greeted by the usual patrons.

She smiled and hugged her way through the crowd to the bar. She was greeted with her usual Long Island Iced Tea as she approached.

"You blessin' us tonight?" Rashawn, the bartender, asked with a smile.

"Yeah, I just finished writing one," Jess responded.

Just then she heard, "I see you back there, Queen. I know you got one for us tonight. I can see by the way you sippin' that drink."

The crowd turned and responded with encouraging cheers as Jess made her way up to the stage. She exchanged greetings with Khani, the host, as the band played.

"I won't lie ya'll, it's been a rough week," Jess began, "so the only way to get through was to write. This one is called Moving On."

The audience responded in agreement and understanding, then fell quiet to listen to her words.

"I'm starting to think maybe I'm crazy
I mean
Why am I expected to be upset with a
man for not being who I wanted him to be?
Clearly he wasn't for me so why should I
engulf my mind in a sea of uncertainty
Claiming it to be...closure
But what is closure?
The way I see it's a yearning for a do-over
To see if it's really over
Like did he really mean to hurt me?

But see no matter what answers I receive
I know I'll still be left feeling less than the
beautiful being I know me to be
So why not just let bygones be bygones
and move on with peace?
I refuse to have continued beef with someone
who was never meant for me
I hear my ancestors speak
Though sometimes I don't want to listen
But when I do...man...I see everything that I felt missing
That's when I have a releasing of all animosity
And I'm able to move about my life clear and filled
with peace
But I have people doubting me
Because I'm not following social rules to
drop clues to his next girl about what we used to do
But again why?
I say let that man live his life
I'm dope enough to know someone better for me
is out there
And it's okay that I wasn't what he wanted or needed
I'm relieved of a burden that could have been
the recipe for certain demise of my positive energy
Time would've continued and I would
have grown resentful
Trying to live to be what he wanted
which is far from who I really am
With that logic I'm able to move on and remain real cool
I don't burn unnecessary bridges cuz the internet
told me to
It's easier to be happy in me than to worry
about a past dude
It's over so let's move on...I say all of this
to encourage you
Find peace in the future and leave the past where it lies

Love will find you with that soul meant to be intertwined
Trust the process and don't waste any more time."

Chapter Two
Day One

Jess turned around as she heard the bells on the front door of her family's African Spirituality shop, Motherland, ring in chaotic harmony.

"I'll be with you in ju-" Jess paused, and a frown covered her face and her heart rate picked up.

"You blocked me without letting me explain," Erick said as he walked toward her.

Jess turned and looked to the back room where her mother was surely listening. She stepped toward Erick and pulled his arm to follow her to the door he'd just entered.

"Not here and not now," she whispered sharply.

"When and where then?" Erick responded, not whispering.

"We don't have anything to talk about. We haven't even been together a year and I'm catching drama about you," Jess said.

"I told you my ex be trippin'."

"You really came all the way over here to give me that generic 'my ex be trippin' line?" Jess paused and rolled her eyes, "Like, *really*?"

"It's not a line if it's true. I'm not with her. She can't stand to see me happy so she plays these games," Erick said looking deeply into her eyes.

Jess disconnected from his gaze, "She only has the access you've allowed. If you wanted it to be over you would've blocked her, but you didn't. I blocked you to cut that access you had to me," she paused and opened the door, "Since you didn't seem to understand what that meant let me tell you clearly. We are done. Please don't try and contact me and don't come back here unless you're making a purchase because I will never stop my coins…so spend or leave!"

Erick looked at Jess and shook his head, "And you wonder why you're single," he said as he turned and walked out.

"I'll be single forever if my other option is you," and with that, she closed the door and walked to the back where she knew her mother would be waiting.

Sitting at the small round table in the middle of the room, Mama Copeland sipped her tea and patted the seat next to her. Jess obediently sat down.

"You okay, baby?" Mama Copeland asked as she lit the lavender incense sitting on the table.

"Honestly, not really," Jess replied. She could feel the tears welling in her eyes, "I thought this would be different."

Her mother poured a cup of tea from the antique set that sat before them and pushed the cup in front of her daughter.

"It's better you saw it now than after years of tears," she said, placing her hand on Jess's shoulder.

Her mother was right, and it was better she stepped away now. It didn't mean that it didn't hurt any less. As she found peace in being single and happy, Erick stepped into the shop with the perfect words and the matching actions that seemed to follow. She felt so comfortable with him. He seemed to be everything she'd been praying for.

Until he wasn't.

So now she sat in her mother's arms crying, releasing frustration and pain. Jess couldn't get the closure she wanted. She wanted this to have never happened and for Erick to have set boundaries from the beginning, never allowing anyone the power he granted these other women with his attention.

She would never have that because the past could not be altered. It was set in her mind as a solid fixture in her history.

Moving on was easier said than done. Jess wanted to brush her shoulders off and keep it moving with her head held high, but her heart ached.

"Seven days," Mama Copeland said, breaking Jess's thoughts.

Jess sighed, understanding her mother's assignment.

Mama Copeland told Jess many heartbreaks ago to only allow someone to consume her energy for seven days. She said to go through the grieving process was expected and needed.

So for seven days she was encouraged to feel everything. From heartache to anger to regret to sadness to guilt. She even included those moments of that temporary passive phase. You know, when you claim you don't care because they lost out when they lost you, only to be punching the air on the inside, ready to crumble at the very thought of them. All of those emotions were encouraged. Mama Copeland said these are natural, and only after these emotions were felt could true acceptance begin.

The key, though, was to never let it consume you beyond that set time. After the seven days she said to pick up the pieces and start working on how to heal and grow. Only with proper care to a wound can one be left with little to no scarring. She needed to be complete within herself if there was hope for true love. No one should ever "complete" her. Mama Copeland believed that the best love was when two whole beings united, allowing an overflow of the love they have in them.

These were powerful words, and Jess yearned to have that kind of love. Her mother knew it with her father, who passed away when Jess was a teenager. Their love was one you read about in books or saw on movie screens. He treated her mother like a Queen, and she honored him like a King.

Jess's father spoiled her in that he demonstrated what a man in love looked like. He showed what a leader is, and her mother showed what true submission is. It was nothing like what was portrayed on social media. It wasn't a servant/ruler dynamic. Instead, it was a peace and understanding between two souls destined for a lifetime together. It was respect, honor, passion, and love. It was beautiful.

Jess wondered if she would ever be able to feel that. She imagined it was possible because she'd witnessed it but often wondered if the men of her generation were just different.

It would take some time before she would allow herself to be vulnerable again. The pain was too great. Jess was tired of grieving. She wanted to be happy.

"Seven days, starting today," Jess whispered to Mama Copeland.

The bells on the front door jingled, and Mama Copeland stood to leave.

Jess grabbed her mother's hand, "Thank you, mama."

Her appreciation was answered with a gentle smile.

Jess sat and sipped her tea. She couldn't believe she had found herself in this position again. This wasn't the first time she sat in the back room of Motherland sipping tea wondering where she'd gone wrong.

"Why do I keep attracting these types of men?" Jess said into the universe.

She paused and waited, expecting an answer, then sighed in the silence.

Seven days.

If only she had taken Mahogany up on the offer to go to Jamaica with her. Jess guessed it was for the best because

Mahogany seemed to have needed this alone time. Maybe that's what she needed too. Some alone time.

Seven days.

Jess walked over to her small cloth book bag on the couch against the wall and pulled out her notebook. The only way she knew how to begin to heal was to write.

The hardest thing I ever thought I would do
is walk away from you
From day one I thought you'd be my day one
but instead I'm here at day one of getting over you
Now I'm here writing poetry about you
I really believed you were a different type of dude
And I'd have no worries when it came to you
But you proved me to be a fool
A fool falling in love and allowing my life to be consumed
By what I imagined would be the start of a beautiful garden's bloom
But what I thought was beauty has turned to ashes because of what you decided to do
Disregarding the conversations of heartbreak that over my head still loomed
I trusted you
But I blamed me because I saw a future groom
And thought I could remove any bad and groom you into a man any woman would want to pursue
And they did so then my one became two
As you did what so many men do
And only thought of you
So now my day one of forever is now day one of healing from you-

"Jess," Mama Copeland said breaking Jess's stride, "I need help out here."

Jess put her pen in her notebook and closed it. She sighed. Though her work was not complete, her therapy had begun, and she felt a slight weight lifted from her shoulders as she placed the notebook back in her bag.

"Coming, mama," she said as she took another deep breath and headed out to face day one of her journey of healing.

Chapter Three
A Good Day

Jess woke up and stretched, smiling as the sun shone through her window. It was a beautiful day, just as she'd prayed for. She believed words were spells, so she spoke into the universe that she would sleep peacefully and arise refreshed.

Since beginning her seven day journey of healing from the heartbreak of another failed relationship, Jess had been dealing with a rollercoaster of emotions. One moment she would feel anger for wasted time, then the next, she'd feel like wasted time was better than no time. She felt lonely. This was rare because Jess could always feel a second presence around her.

Jess had a twin sister, Justina, in the womb that transitioned before experiencing this world. Though she never knew her in the physical world, she'd always felt her in the spiritual. Loneliness didn't seem to exist in Jess's world, but it was her living reality over the past few days.

She realized that the loneliness wasn't from losing Erick. Instead, it was just the thought of being alone. She was turning thirty this November, and the idea of not even a potential mate was scary for the first time. Jess had lived in her ability to be alone. She was strong, black, and independent. She never intended to be so independent that it left her with a Single relationship status on her tax forms.

Once her father passed, she and her mother had to learn how to manage on their own. No, they weren't left helpless, but there were things that her father just...did. Simple things that didn't feel so simple once he was gone. Like taking out the trash and getting the oil changed. Yes, she and mom were capable, but as a Daddy's Girl and her mother as a Queen, they never had to.

Jess yearned for that male presence in her life so she could put down the load she was forced to bare by circumstance and allow him to pick it up. The problem was that many men saw her handling life and assumed she had no desire to submit. She did, though. She wanted a man to lead her through this journey of life. However, Jess didn't understand how men who had no idea what direction they were traveling in expected her to allow them to take that lead.

So here she was. Alone. Feeling lonely.

The evening before she tossed and turned while she thought about the what ifs. What if she hadn't given Erick her phone number? What if she had just ignored Tia and seen where things would go? What if he was telling the truth, and she was just causing problems to break them up? What if she won?

Jess had to get out of bed and clear the negative energy that had overrun her home. She turned on her playlist of the sounds of water and began to breathe as she slowly sat down on the floor and crossed her legs. She needed to move through her emotions so she could come out of this with a lesson learned. Mama Copeland always told Jess that wasted time only begins when things go uncorrected. This was her time of correction.

After her moment of meditation, Jess found herself in a blissful rest. Her mattress seemed to fold around her body and tuck her into a deep sleep. When she awoke, she felt refreshed.

Day seven. The last day she'd allow Erick to enter her thoughts and reside rent-free. There was an eviction notice nailed to the front door of her mind. She would not let the fear of being alone consume her because she knew she'd be okay. There was someone out there for her. She just needed a moment to breathe and figure out the proper frequency to draw in the compatible spirit she desired.

After a moment of admiring the sun's shine, Jess got up to put on a kettle of water for her morning tea. The universe was speaking to her, and she could hear it clearly. She walked to the bathroom and allowed the water to boil.

Jess looked in the mirror and smiled. She'd written a piece a few years ago that she recited on mornings like this.

She began the way she always had as if reciting to a crowd of her emotions, "Please don't just read. I need you to say this one with me."

Jess took a deep breath,

"Today is going to be a good day
I proclaim
I woke up on time
Had memories of a pleasant dream on my mind
I looked in the mirror to find beauty staring back at me
There are no traces of negative energy and insecurity
I walked back to my room and fell on my knees
And thanked The Universe in advance for what's to be
I opened my window to find with no surprise

That there's not a cloud in the sky
Again I must say
I proclaim
Today is going to be a good day!"

Jess smiled at her reflection, "Now that you've said it take the time to believe it."

*****

Mama Copeland greeted Jess with a list of things to do as she entered Motherland.

"Hi, mama," Jess responded with a smile.

"Hey, Jess," Mama Copeland said flatly in her direction and then half-smiled a greeting to the next customer at the cash register.

The shop was busy this morning, so she understood why her mother was relieved to have her walk through the door, even if she was late.

"Sorry I'm late, I picked up some breakfast on the way in. I didn't realize we were jumpin' like this today."

"You'd know if you were here on time. Niecy will be here at noon," Mama Copeland replied as she handed the customer her receipt.

Niecy was like a younger sister to Jess. Mama Copeland took her under her wing when she was fourteen years old. Her parents weren't exactly the most significant examples of stability. Niecy's mother seemed more concerned with her new boyfriends than her child. Her father loved Niecy dearly but was serving time in prison on a marijuana conviction.

She'd become family, so it was only natural that she would be a part of Motherland as well. The only problem was that Niecy was not a morning person, so opening was never an option. They could schedule her, but she would never show up on time.

That was why Jess was usually there to open and why her mother's aura displayed pure annoyance at her late arrival.

Jess maneuvered through the shop toward the back room, "Let me put this down and I'll get started."

She returned a moment later with a box of books ready to be shelved. Her mind focused on the task at hand, moving quickly as she heard the bell chime with every customer that entered and exited. Lost in her work, Jess's mind began to drift into a peaceful rhythm.

"What up, Long Island," Jess heard from behind as she propped the last book in its place.

She smiled and turned around to the familiar voice, "I'mma change my name to that one day cuz I'm starting to get used to it."

Jess and Rashawn laughed lightly as they embraced in a hug.

"What brings you in here today?"

Rashawn's face lit up, "My sister is graduating high school. 4.0 GPA," he added with pride, "I'm trying to find something for her. "

Jess's smile brightened, "That's dope," she replied, "Follow me. I have the perfect thing."

Rashawn followed Jess to an area filled with stones and crystals. She picked up a rose gold necklace and held it out.

"It's a Rose Quartz crystal. Among other things it helps manifest prosperity," she explained as she placed it in the palm of his hand.

"Yeah, I like this," he smiled as he examined the piece.

"I told you I had the perfect gift," she smiled slyly.

They exchanged another look.

"Are you almost finished because I need help up here," Mama Copeland said, cutting their stare.

"Yes, ma'am," Jess called back.

She looked at Rashawn and shrugged an unspoken, *Gotta go*. He nodded and followed her to the line.

Mama Copeland made it a point to ring him up herself when Rashawn's turn arrived. She remained pleasant as he stole glances at Jess while she helped the last customer gather their bags.

Once the store was empty, Mama Copeland took a seat at the table that held her room temperature biscuits and picked one up.

Pointing with the biscuit, Mama Copeland gestured for Jess's attention. Jess walked over and stood by the door.

"You need a minute to catch your breath before you take on another marathon," she said.

Jess knew her mother, so no deeper explanation was needed, "I'm not doing anything. Today is day seven, and I'm just at peace right now."

"Be careful allowing your peace to be defined by filling a void," she paused, "I saw the way you and that young man were flirting."

"Mama, he's the bartender at the open mic I go to."

"What's that got to do with ya'll flirting?" Mama Copeland asked.

"We weren't flirting," Jess said, sighing.

Her mother looked at her as if peering into her soul.

"Well it was harmless flirting," Jess conceded.

"Harmless for who?"

"For everyone," Jess said, "I'm not going to jump into anything else right now. I promise."

Mama Copeland bit into her biscuit, "You don't have to promise me anything. Just be careful is all I'm saying. You're still healing. The seven days is not to dwell in it, but it doesn't mean you've completely gotten over your feelings. You need to sort that out before you even 'harmlessly flirt'," she said with air quotes.

"I get it and you're right," Jess responded.

"I know," her mother said with a grin.

Jess admired her mother's discernment. She knew she was blessed to have a woman like that in her life. Rashawn was cool, but she really wasn't seeking anything but harmless flirtations with him.

But her mother was right. Healing was a process, and the last thing she needed was to distract from it. Tomorrow would begin a new day. She was single again, and she needed time to embrace it. That would be the only way for her to reach her true point of peace.

Jess's alert went off. One new follower. She smiled and tapped the picture. He *was* fine though.

Chapter Four
Imaginings

Jess's phone buzzed on the coffee table in her living room. She paused the television show she was barely watching when she realized it was from Mahogany.

Girl! I just told him I love him.

Jess choked on the smoke she had just inhaled and almost dropped her phone with the tightly rolled marijuana blunt she held in her opposite hand.

OMG! What did he say?????

She waited impatiently as the text bubble popped up on her screen. Mahogany was in Jamaica trying to regain her focus so she could begin to paint again. She'd traded her brushes for computer programs after she graduated college and was living the life society expected of her, complete with the acceptable man. However, her journey began when she had a moment of clarity and avoided marrying a man she was never meant to be with, in Jess's opinion. After that moment Mahogany began to feel a passion for her true gift again.

While looking for a muse to inspire work for her upcoming art exhibit hosted by her well known artistic family, she found a man named Tavis. He seemed to be everything any woman would dream of, but Mahogany had made it clear that it was a vacation fling. It was a much needed release not meant to go beyond the island. So Jess was shocked when she read the text talking about love.

Her phone buzzed in her hand.

Nothing!
He just went in the bathroom.

Jess put her hand to her mouth in disbelief. She was speechless. All she could manage was a "wow" emoji.

Mahogany responded quickly.

Exactly! I just want him to leave. I'm soooo embarrassed.

Jess's phone alerted her to a social media post. She opened the app to see Rashawn tagged Motherland and Jess, specifically, in a reaction video to his sister receiving the necklace she'd recommended. The Rose Quartz stone sat in the rose gold necklace that rested beautifully on the young lady's sandy brown skin.

Jess smiled as she thought about Rashawn. He was extremely handsome in the video. She had never been blind to his looks. He just never approached her romantically, so she continued to treat him as just a cool bartender she knew from Verse One.

Rashawn always had a Long Island Iced Tea, Jess's usual drink, ready for her whenever she entered the establishment. They would exchange small talk and a few laughs, but that was it. When he walked into her shop, she'd realized they'd never seen each other in the daylight. As fine as he was behind the bar in the dimly lit café, he was a whole work of art in the sunlight.

Jess shook her head to remove the thoughts that began to creep into her mind. She closed the app and went back to the text message thread.

Well do u? Jess wondered if her friend was caught in a moment or if she had truly found love on a week's vacation.

It doesn't even matter. I won't see him again after tomorrow.

Jess's heart broke for Mahogany. She could feel the embarrassment and fear of rejection in each word she read.

U okay? Jess asked.

Girl, I'm trippin'! Mahogany replied.

Jess responded with a sad face emoji.

Mahogany answered with a crying emoji.

You probably just caught him off guard. Give him the night. Jess tried to ease her friend's mind. She didn't want her whole reason for going to Jamaica interrupted by an unexpected heartbreak.

Jess waited a moment and watched the text bubble start and stop until the phone buzzed again.

I'm going to sleep.
Good night, boo...

Jess sighed. She hoped that things would work out and Mahogany would get what she was looking for out of this vacation. Jess looked forward to the paintings she was sure Mahogany would produce once she got out of this funk. Even the tug at her heartstrings, whether good or bad, could serve as a muse for her work. Mahogany would be okay, and Jess rested in knowing that.

But would *she*? Jess had just left a relationship and found herself longing for another man. It was bad enough she had that one night stand with Mr. "M" only days after leaving Erick, but Rashawn was too good of a guy for her to just have a sexual relationship with. She wasn't even going to try and fool herself. She would definitely develop feelings at one touch from that man. So all she could do was leave those thoughts in her imagination.

Jess took a final hit of her blunt, placed it in the ashtray, and began writing.

My mind battles
As I try and tackle
The pounding of my pulse
Attraction and lust
Right now I can't trust myself with you
Our astrological signs align on a carnal vibe
But I've decided not to even try
But my desires break through and fight
The scent of your cologne, so slight
Filled me as you touched me
Innocently
I now lay with imaginings
Visions of you and me doing things
Unimaginably nasty –

A knock interrupted Jess's thought. She exhaled and put her notebook and pen down.

"Who is it," she spoke loudly through the closed door.

"Marcus," came a familiar voice, "I'm sorry to just pop up but I left my watch and I never got your number."

Marcus! *That* was his name! She opened the door and smiled.

"It's okay," she said, "Come in."

Marcus followed Jess into her apartment, "Everything good with you?"

She smiled and turned to him, "It's better now."

Jess walked him over to the couch and sat down first, gesturing him to sit next to her.

"Are you busy," he said in observation of her untidy gathering of marijuana paraphernalia and half empty pages of incomplete thoughts.

"Yeah, but I can take a break," she responded, "I'm about to roll up again anyway."

She pulled out her jar of marijuana and began the process.

"So what you been up to?" Marcus asked as he got comfortable.

"Nothing much," Jess replied as she began to break down the large nugget she pulled out of the jar, "Keeping busy with my writing and working."

"You're a writer?"

"Yup," she replied as she began rolling the marijuana in the leaf.

"Spit something."

Without hesitation, Jess began,

"Damn…look at you over there just long brown and thick
Damn…Let me just say from the beginning that,
um, I'm really just tryna hit
See…you are undeniably the sexiest thing I've
seen this evening
I smelled you when I walked in and I felt a tingling
Lingering
So tempting
Only problem I see is that you're here with
somebody else
Damn…
You see I do believe you'd be better with me…
If I do say so myself
I inhale the scent of your being and you…
Take me somewhere else…
Wow
Now
Honestly I'd compromise
And share this one time
Let you come inside
While she stares in my eyes

Yeah I just might
Your soul is tied to me
Captured in a natural leaf
You bring peace to me
He or she
You ease my anxiety
Violet indigo indica
Illustrates purple haze
As I gaze
And I call you by your sweet name
Mary Jane."

She smiled as he began to snap his fingers in approval. Jess lit the blunt she had perfectly rolled while speaking her piece. She inhaled the smoke and turned to him, gesturing for him to come closer.

Marcus obeyed as he leaned in and opened his mouth slightly, allowing the partially inhaled smoke to leave her lips and travel between his. They both closed their eyes and inhaled, never moving from their close distance.

Jess smiled and leaned in again, kissing him gently. She touched his wrist where his watch rested, never hidden. She'd noticed it as soon as the door was opened. When he grinned and looked at her in the doorway, they both understood that he was not there to find some lost watch.

Jess had left him craving her, and in the moment of sexual thoughts of Rashawn, she felt Marcus's timing couldn't have been better. She needed a release, and Rashawn wasn't an option. Not yet. But Marcus...she'd make sure to remember his name after this one. Their unspoken understanding began a fluid conversation that would last all night.

Chapter Five
Peace

When you tap into the energy that lives beneath the skin deep
You will find that frequency of peace
I encourage you to love you
Because even your flaws are beautiful
You are a one-of-a-kind masterpiece
And if you want to fall in love beyond skin deep
First, fall in love with your inner peace

    Jess put down her high school notebook that held her younger thoughts and inhaled deeply. She smiled as she exhaled. Since her father's passing, she desired a sense of inner peace. There was a void that was in her heart. Her father's loss felt different than her sister's. Though she could sometimes feel him, it wasn't like her sister. Justina seemed to *live* in her. Their spirits being one. She missed her father so much, and sometimes she wondered if her strong desire for a man was somehow an attempt to fill that void.

    She set high expectations because she knew what love looked like. She wanted what she wanted and despite what social media would have people believe, she knew that with patience she could have it. Patience was key though, and that was the hard part. Jess knew she needed to take her time, but sometimes she felt like time was running out.

    "Jess!" Niecy yelled as she walked through the front door of Motherland.

Jess quickly put down her notebook and looked up, "What's up?"

"Girl," Niecy paused and then shook her head, continuing as she walked to the back to put down her keys and purse. When she emerged she had her phone in hand, "So I was bored last night and scrollin' through online, and I saw a pic of Erick and some girl."

Jess rolled her eyes, "Block him Niecy." She did not want weekly reports on what was going on in this man's life.

"I already did," she answered quickly, "but before all that I got curious so you know me…" she let her voice trail off.

"What did you do?" Jess asked.

"I wanted to know who she was so I put on my detective hat."

Jess shook her head in disbelief. At the same time she was in total belief because this was who Niecy was. This new generation was relentless when it came to snooping. They all needed to join the FBI as far as Jess was concerned.

Niecy continued, "If this is the same chick, then she was tellin' you the truth. They been together for like five years. They even got a kid together," she looked at the phone and read the name. *Tia*

Jess's eyes widen. Erick had never mentioned having a child. One thing about Jess, she was not interested in dating a man with kids. It wasn't that she didn't like kids, but she wanted her first child to be the father's first child too. Jess had expressed this to him early in their relationship, and he'd said he understood. Then he told her he didn't have any children.

"Yeah, that's her," Jess said quietly, shaking her head in disbelief, "He denied his child?"

"I'm sorry, sis. I just thought you should know so you can stop thinkin' 'bout him cuz clearly he ain't shit," Niecy said, walking to Jess and putting her arm around her.

Jess fought back the tears, disappointed that he could still evoke that emotion from her.

"You wanna see her?"

Against her better judgment, Jess took the phone.

"She ain't even cute," Niecy said as she looked on with Jess.

Whether Tia was cute or not was irrelevant because clearly she was cute enough for him.

Jess stared at the picture of the happy family. She felt a sense of relief in that first moment. She had let him go. It was a bad look on so many levels. Not only was he breaking her heart, but he also had to be ripping apart the very soul of this woman. He denied their child. What kind of a man did that?

"Trashy ass," Niecy said.

"It's like you read my mind," Jess replied as she handed the phone back.

"I know you did your seven days. I hope I ain't set you back," Niecy said gently.

"Surprisingly, no," Jess said, "I'm good. Mama said it's better it happened sooner rather than later, and I agree. I can't imagine being years into it and finding out I'm the jump off."

"You weren't the jump off, sis."

"As much as I hate to say it, I was. She's been around before me and they have a whole family situation."

"I wonder why she ain't just tell you what was going on," Niecy scrolled through her phone as she spoke.

"She might be embarrassed," Jess said, "Hell, *I'd* be if I was dealing with a man like him."

"Truuuue," Niecy exaggerated.

"Besides, I never really gave her the chance. The first time he was with me and the second time I blocked them."

The conversation drifted off and they started their routine of tidying up the shop and restocking items. They found their rhythm, and Jess's mind began to drift.

A part of her was shocked at Niecy's discovery, but a bigger part was filled with disappointment in herself. She knew something wasn't right. Yeah, she thought he was cheating, but she thought Erick was cheating on her. She never imagined he was cheating on someone else with her! Jess shook her head at the thought. She was the side chick.

"I talked to my daddy," Niecy said from the corner of the shop.

Jess perked up, "Really? How's he doing in there?"

Niecy's father, Clarence, was arrested with a little less than an ounce of marijuana and was sentenced to ten years in prison because they threw a distribution charge in there. It was a part of this country's politics that Jess hated. As an American-born citizen, Jess loved this country, but sometimes it had a way of making that hard to do.

"He's chillin'," the hesitation could be heard clearly in her pause, "I mean as much as he can in that hell."

Jess nodded in agreement, "I can't believe his little girl is turning 21 this weekend."

Niecy smiled, "Yeah, he said he's gettin' old and I told him I agree."

They both laughed.

"So what do you have planned? I'm sure there will be a lot of drinking," Jess said with a knowing smile.

"Hella *drankin'*!" Niecy said with an excited giggle, "Cuz *drinkin'* will *not* be enough!"

"Oh lawd," Jess responded, matching her energy.

"You should come."

"I'm there!"

"Good," Niecy said, "We can find you a good man."

Jess shook her head, "Nope. I'm good on that."

"You know somebody is gonna come along, right?"

"Yeah, but at this point I wonder if I'd even recognize it if it did," Jess responded.

"My daddy always tells me that every day his goal is to be a better man than he was the day before. He said he does that because he wants to make sure he is the best version of himself when he gets out and we get real time together."

"That's dope," Jess replied with a smile.

"Yeah it is. But what's even more *dope*," Niecy said playfully mocking Jess, "is that even though he's in prison he's still an example of what kind of man I want in my life."

They both paused as Niecy allowed it to sink in.

She continued, "Mama Copeland always says that we tend to find men like our fathers. I always wondered if that meant I'd end up with a prison bae or somethin'," she laughed lightly, "But then I realized that I was focusin' on *where* he was and not *who* he was. And who my daddy is, is a man that wants to be a good person because he wants the best for me. The way I see it, any man that wants to be with me gotta be the best version of himself so he can be healthy for my energy."

Jess smiled a Niecy. She was wise beyond her years and she knew a lot of that came from how much Niecy looked up to Mama Copeland. Any time Mama Copeland provided a thought, or even so much as an idea, Niecy would take it in like it was gospel. Jess always knew she was privileged to have such a wise woman as a mother. She wore that privilege as a badge of honor, especially when she saw the fruits of it, as she had in this moment.

"You're going to find the right one," Niecy smiled, "Better yet, he'll find you. And when he does you'll know it."

Jess used to call Niecy her play sister, but moments like this made her feel like there was nothing "play" about it. Blood could not make them closer, and Jess felt blessed to have her in her life.

"Yeah, you're right," Jess perked her energy up, "But it will *not* be this weekend while I'm with a bunch of drunk twenty-one year olds!"

Niecy laughed, "Fine," she rolled her eyes playfully, "As long as you promise you're coming I won't bother you…this week."

"Then I promise!"

Chapter Six
No Rush

Niecy's words from earlier that day lingered in Jess's mind as she dressed and headed to Verse One. Everything she said was right. Jess deserved someone that was the best version of themselves. She had fallen for facades one too many times, and she was tired.

Jess didn't want to believe that all men were bad. She and Niecy's fathers were examples of that. They were two totally different men in every way, proving that good men not only existed, but they didn't come in just one form.

Jess knew it wasn't a matter of *if* a good man would take residence in her heart. Instead, it was up to her to be ready and emotionally capable of recognizing him when he came her way.

Verse One was packed as usual as Jess entered. Rashawn caught her eye immediately and nodded her way. She walked toward him as he began making her drink.

"What up, Long Island," Rashawn greeted as she approached.

Jess smiled and took the drink, "Thank you," she said, taking a sip. Jess took out her credit card to pay.

"I gotchu," he said, waving off her attempt, "You made big bro look good. Just wanted to say thank you."

Jess smiled as she put her card back in her wallet.

"Actually, I was wondering if I can say a real thank you by taking you to dinner-"

He was cut off by Khani's introduction, "Next to bless the mic we have one of our favorites." The regulars verbalized their agreement, knowing without further description who he was calling on.

Jess began to walk toward the stage. Her heart was pounding, but not because of nervousness of presenting another piece, but instead the invitation she had narrowly escaped.

She'd been a customer of Rashawn's for years, but it wasn't until he stepped into her world as a customer at her shop that she suddenly saw him in a different light. Yeah, he'd always been attractive, but Verse One was her neutral zone. His good looks were the last thing on her mind when she frequented. It was her place where her only focus was her art. She could be vulnerable and express herself freely because she had no romantic attachments in there. Jess hadn't even brought Erick to this sacred space. She never wanted memories created that would hurt later. Her heart pounded because, without intention, she had already created a memory with Rashawn.

So when he asked her to dinner all she felt was panic. Overthinking wasn't something she made a habit of, but it was her reality in that moment. In those few seconds, Jess imagined the dinner being super dope, leading to them falling in love eventually and inevitably falling out, causing her safe space to be filled with painful memories. What would she do then? She'd have no choice but to leave Verse One behind, and by the sound of the crowd that welcomed her as she approached the microphone, that was not an option.

"How ya'll doing tonight," she asked in the sultry voice that always seemed to come out when she entered her world of spoken word.

The crowd responded with *Good* and *Alright*.

"Tonight I'm just going to do the first piece that pops in my head, so ride with me.

>I'm trying to go quickly, but I don't wanna rush
>What's between us because it's way more than lust
>With only your touch, you gained my trust
>So now my heart is open
>I thought I was still coping
>From the last one who had my heart against
>the ropes and
>Giving it uppercuts
>But cut to a chapter that's new
>And there's you
>Making me see that my past was worth it
>Because that once insecure girl, you can now
>see as a woman who's confident
>One who looks in her reflections and says,
>"you are beautiful"
>And I hope my words don't frighten you
>But there's a vibe
>One we can't hide
>And as we decide what will be next,
>I've seen in my mind's eye
>What we will be should we decide to coincide
>our emotions and take this ride

The energy we share, I wouldn't dare try and compare
To anyone who used to be here
Because you are unapologetically
Of royalty as I am me
Poised to rule the world, status of King and Queen
We'll be
But then again, we are, and I'm not trynna sugarcoat this
We are the epitome of super dopeness
My goodness
I have to pause to catch my breath
Cuz when I think about you, my pulse refuses to rest
And the rest of the world seems to cease to exist
Only you and I live in it
Even if only for a moment
As I feel bliss
So it's taking everything in me not to rush it
Because we just click
And time will tell if I get to drop that L or will I have to resist it
But I doubt it
Now, of course I'm daydreaming, and so I'mma allow life to take its course and show us our meaning
Though it's hard,
I'll be patient and take our time to be us
Cuz I'm trying to go quickly, but I don't wanna rush."

As Jess finished her piece she felt a black girl blush fill her face. Her light skin allowed for others to see it, but only slightly as her melanin masked the depth of it all. She could feel the heat rise as she found herself looking toward the back by the bar.

The lights that shown on the stage made it impossible for her to see Rashawn's eyes, but their aligned frequencies could be felt. She had no doubt that he felt them too.

Jess stepped down from the stage as the crowd's applause and loud snaps seemed to fade into the background. Suddenly she felt a need to avoid Rashawn. She couldn't say yes to his invitation because she knew there was something there. But was she ready? Not knowing the answer to that question scared her, so she chose avoidance.

*****

Jess was able to sober up faster than any other time she'd left Verse One. That was because she didn't have another drink after the one with Rashawn. Avoiding him meant no more visiting the bar for the evening. It was annoying but necessary.

It all worked out in her favor anyway because Jess needed to be alert for her 5 a.m. pick-up.

"Mahogany!" Jess jumped out of her car as she pulled up in front of the baggage claim door her friend was standing by.

The two hugged as if they hadn't seen each other in months, though it had only been a week. Jess helped Mahogany place her bags in the trunk and they started on their way.

"So tell me everything!" Jess began.

"Nope," Mahogany responded, "You start. What the hell happened with Erick?"

"To be honest it started before you even left."

"WHAT?"

"I didn't want to mess up your vacation before it even began so I just figured I'd deal with it."

"Awe, friend," Mahogany frowned, "I'm sorry."

"It's all good," Jess replied, "I'm honestly fine."

"Mama Copeland's seven days?" Mahogany asked knowingly.

"Yup."

"I won't lie. It helped me when I needed it."

Jess nodded her head in agreement. She then filled her friend in with all the details that followed. Erick coming to the shop, Niecy's investigative work, and the words of wisdom from both Mama Copeland and Niecy. She ended it with Rashawn.

"Wow," Mahogany said when Jess finished, "That's a lot."

They sat in silence for a moment.

"So you're sure you're over Erick?" Mahogany said.

"Yeah. I think the family photo was my final straw. I won't lie and say I'm completely over what he did, but I am over him," Jess replied.

"I get it," Mahogany sighed, "Rashawn is cool, but I think you need to go with your gut. It hasn't even been a full three weeks. You need time."

Even though Mahogany didn't write poetry, she was a known regular at Verse One too. She and Rashawn had fun interactions because, on most visits, Mahogany would simply ask him to surprise her with a drink. Rashawn got a chance to experiment with new drink mixes, and there sparked their relationship.

"Yeah, I'm going to…."Jess's voice trailed off.

"Buuut?" Mahogany asked.

"There's a part of me that wonders if I'm missing out on something good," Jess paused a moment before she continued, "I keep thinking that if I miss out, it would be because of Erick. How many times do I have to see my exes go on to live happily ever after without me getting mine?"

Jess pulled into a parking space in front of Mahogany's building and placed the car in Park.

"I get it. So I'll say this," Mahogany turned toward her friend as she released her seatbelt, "Don't move until you know you're ready. The man that's for you will be there when you are. It may not go how you see it in your mind, but it will happen."

"Listen to you," Jess smiled at her friend, "Maybe I need to go find a muse in Jamaica so I can come back all aligned and shit."

"Maybe you do," Mahogany said with a sly smile.

Jess got serious for a moment, "Thank you."

"Any time."

They both hopped out of the vehicle. As their conversation turned to Mahogany's vacation recap, Jess felt her mind settle a little. In a moment of vulnerable clarity with her best friend, Jess realized she knew what she wanted to do.

And in that same moment, she gave herself permission to do it.

Chapter Seven
Red Dress Occasion

It was a red dress occasion. Jess walked into the restaurant and felt all eyes on her. Perhaps her confidence was causing illusions, but it was how she felt. Beautiful.

Jess was surprised when she saw that Rashawn had already arrived. He approached her with a smile. Her mind drifted into a verse.

> *Issa red dress occasion*
> *No, you are not mistaken*
> *I did this on purpose*
> *For us*
> *On this read dress occasion*

"Jess," Rashawn greeted.

"No Long Island?"

Rashawn grinned, "Nah, not tonight."

Jess wondered if this connection existed before their encounter at Motherland. She didn't think so, but her energy responded to even the sight of him. He was beyond average attractive, but that wasn't it. It was the way he moved, his...swag.

Rashawn pulled out Jess's chair and allowed her to sit.

"You look beautiful," he said.

"Thank you," she replied.

Using my curves as persuasion
For you to give me you
My attitude is quite subdued
But inside, I know this might be dangerous
Using this red dress as temptation

Their gaze broke as their menus were placed in front of them. They both smiled a thank you and locked eyes again.

"I didn't think you'd hit me up," Rashawn said, "After you finished your piece you avoided me the rest of the night."

"I did," Jess admitted, "I didn't know how to answer."

I gotta keep it cool though
My body says yes, but my mind is saying hell no
Slow down lil mama
Exhale and relax lil mama
This is your world...Period no comma

"Why's that?"

"Well," Jess picked up her menu and glanced over it momentarily. Finally, she cleared her throat and looked up from the menu, "I just got out of a relationship. I didn't know if it would be too much."

Rashawn raised his eyebrows, "Really?"

"Why is that so surprising?"

"I've just never seen you with anybody at Verse One."

Jess nodded her head in understanding, "To be honest, I guess I always knew something was off. That's my sacred space so I don't bring just anyone," she paused a moment, "It's a public space and he knew that's where I was so if he wanted to come he could have...but on his own."

"Sheesh," Rashawn replied with a slight grin.

"What?" Jess said with a confused laugh.

"You just left that man at home."

Jess laughed, "That does sound harsh, huh?"

"Just a lil' bit," Rashawn laughed while demonstrating with his thumb and first finger held close together.

"Well, I'm not trying to be. It's just I need my space to be vulnerable, you know?"

Rashawn nodded, "I get it," he paused a moment, "So, if you don't mind...what happened?"

"What always happens?"

"He cheated."

"Ding! Ding! Ding!" Jess responded, as if he'd won a prize.

Rashawn shook his head, "Damn, I'm sorry that happened to you. Though I won't lie, I'm grateful it's over," he looked at Jess, "It *is* over right?"

"I wouldn't be here if it wasn't," she replied, "I'm good. Like I said, as I look back I realize something was always off."

Their conversation took a pause as they ordered their meals.

Jess continued, "But enough about my past. What about you? I'm assuming you would label yourself as single, but do you have a baby mama or someone that wouldn't agree with that status?"

Rashawn laughed, maybe a bit louder than he intended, "Nah, I don't have any kids and I don't lead women on."

It was Jess's turn to raise her eyebrow.

Rashawn took a sip of his wine, "I'm not saying I never have, but I'm thirty-two now. I'm a little too old to be out here in these streets. Plus I'm anti-STD. Nah, I'm good."

"Oh, you are *not* lying about these crazy diseases," Jess said as her face relaxed, "So no children? No maybe babies?"

"Zero," Rashawn squinted his eyes, "You don't like kids?"

"I love them," Jess answered, "It's just that I want my first to be his first so we can have that experience together. I have nothing against anyone that doesn't feel the same way, I'm just saying, for me."

"I get it."

"I've been lied to about that before," saying it out loud stung Jess a bit, but it was a reality.

Rashawn paused a moment, "Well, if I did I'd never hide it. I'm the youngest of five and all my siblings have kids that love their Uncle Shawn," he paused again, "and if I'm to be honest, ya boy was lame as hell for that."

"Agreed," Jess said with a smile and slight exhale.

Their conversation continued through their appetizers, main course, and dessert. The evening felt good and perfect. Everything in Jess screamed that this was a good thing and that relaxing was okay.

But it was hard to relax when she'd just gotten out of a situation where her trust was broken. She didn't want to make Rashawn, or anyone else, suffer because of what one man did. Jess realized she had to take her time with this one if she wanted it to become anything.

This was their first date, so she didn't need to think too deeply about it, but she did need to remain intentional with her decisions. In this moment, that meant saying good night as the evening ended.

But why he gotta smell so good?
And looking like the assignment was understood
Damn, I'm feeling a slight condensation
And a bit of a sensation
But I can't give into this temptation
Well not yet
So I'mma leave him with physical elevation from
the memories of this red dress occasion

*****

Jess turned the key in her door and stepped inside. Her date with Rashawn was perfect. She damn near wanted to spin around like she was in a movie. Instead, she sat on her couch and began to roll up.

Her phone rang, and she answered, knowing who it was without looking.

"Soooo," Mahogany said into the screen, "I didn't get any 'save me' texts so I'm assuming it was good."

"It was perfect," Jess said.

"Hold up let's have a session," Mahogany said as she picked up her pre-rolled blunt and lit it.

Jess followed suit.

"So tell me everything," Mahogany continued as she exhaled a cloud of smoke.

"He was the perfect gentleman. I mean, like, real grown man vibes," Jess started.

Jess was so hyped up from the date that she needed to get it all out so she could relax, and a recap was precisely what was required. Mahogany smiled and nodded as she got the moment by moment details.

"So do you think you'll go out again?"

"Definitely," Jess answered, "I'm just moving *real* smooth on this one. I think I like him, but I know it's really soon.

I followed my heart, but I'm not going to be dumb about it and rush anything.

"Well that's the smart route."

"See, ya girl is growing," Jess said with a slight giggle.

When Jess was attracted she was known to just go full speed ahead, throwing caution to the wind. She wanted this to be different, so she knew she had to move differently.

Their call ended, but Jess's energy was still on ten and she needed it at a cool six or seven.

As seven approached she heard a knock on her door. Though she behaved with Rashawn, her body still wanted what it wanted. So as she sat in the back of her rideshare earlier, she sent a text that would surely get her through the night.

"So is this going to be a habit?" Marcus said with a grin.

"It can be," Jess responded.

She led him into her apartment and to her bed. Thoughts of Rashawn flashed in her mind as she released her sexual frustrations on Marcus. She'd take her time with her heart, but she would allow her body to be satisfied in the meantime.

Chapter Eight
Melanated Queen

Oxtail over rice, baked macaroni and cheese, collard greens, yams, and cornbread sat on the table as Mama Copeland apologized for not making a *full* dinner for Niecy's birthday.

"I just had so much going on at the shop this week," she said as she returned with a big pitcher of freshly made sweet tea.

Jess, Niecy, and Mahogany smiled in unison as they stared at the steaming hot food placed before them. They glanced at each other, speaking with their eyes. *If this isn't a full dinner, I don't know what is.*

"This dinner is perfect, Mama Copeland," Niecy said.

"Well at least I have my girls with me in one place. Between the traveling," she looked at Mahogany and then Niecy, "and growing up, I just can't keep up with you two."

"Well my schedule has freed up and I've reset. I'll be by to get my dinners again," Mahogany said with a slight giggle.

"How was your trip anyway?" Mama Copeland asked Mahogany.

"It was beautiful. The water, the sand, the music –"

"The men," Jess interjected with a sly grin.

Mahogany playfully cut her eyes at her friend, "The *people*."

"Well," Mama Copeland said as she sat down, "just remember to focus on your priorities. Don't let *people* keep you from reaching your goal. You went down to Jamaica to find your muse so you can come back and have a reason for leaving the well paying job you had," that last comment being said with a little more emphasis.

"Yes ma'am," Mahogany replied, "I had fun, but I definitely accomplished my goal. I can't wait for you all to see what I'm working on."

"Good," Mama Copeland said. She turned to Niecy, "And you."

"Ma'am?" Niecy said.

"In a couple hours you'll be twenty-one," Mama Copeland smiled.

"Ayyyyye!" Niecy replied with a giggle.

"I remember when you first started coming around," Mama Copeland began, "You were so rebellious...and that *mouth*," she paused and shook her head, "to see you now though. So respectful, so loving, so wise...wise beyond your years."

Jess and Mahogany looked on and smiled.

Mama Copeland continued, "The number two represents balance and the number one represents new beginnings. So as you turn twenty-one you will want to seek balance as you enter your new phase of life. You should welcome experiences of freedom in love and relationships. And not just romantic relationships, but family and friends as well."

All three ladies sat and took in every word. When Mama Copeland spoke wisdom it was like being fed, and they all wanted their bellies filled.

"Practice thinking before you act in order to make wise decisions. Now is truly the time when those of us who have seen you grow will witness if it all stuck. Did you learn? Which lessons will you apply to your life?" Mama Copeland paused again, resting her hand gently on Niecy's, " Make us proud."

Niecy smiled at Mama Copeland, "Yes ma'am."

Everyone began to dish out their food and eat. The ladies continued with their conversation as the clanking of serving spoons against dishes filled the room.

"I talked to my daddy today," Niecy said with a bright smile.

"Oh, yeah?" Mahogany replied, "How's he doing?"

"He's cool," Niecy turned her attention to Mama Copeland, "He said to thank you for being there for me all these years."

Mama Copeland smiled.

Niecy continued, "I really do appreciate it, Mama Copeland. Like, I know my mama loves me, but I ain't never been a priority for her. My daddy loves me, but..." her voice trailed out.

Mama Copeland stopped eating and touched Niecy's hand again.

Niecy smiled, "I miss him every day, but when I'm around you I feel like I got my mama and daddy in one."

"Awe," Jess said, breaking the moment as Mahogany nudged her friend.

Niecy was fun and had a big spirit, but she wasn't often sentimental. By the time she came into their lives, she had hardened. She was forced to be an adult to her mother while trying to understand why her father wasn't around. She had so many conflicting emotions that she'd just shut down. It took a long time before she understood that her mother was sick beyond a daughter's help, and her father was locked up because of a system created to keep black men down. She had softened a bit since the day she became a part of the family. However, she still left little room for actual vulnerability either. A moment like this, when she opened up about her feelings, was refreshing.

"Well I love you baby," Mama Copeland said, "And happy birthday!"

They hugged as Jess got up and went to her small bookbag on the couch. She pulled out a card and small box and returned to the table.

"Here you go," Jess handed the box and card envelope to Niecy, "Happy birthday."

Niecy opened the card and read out loud,

"Melanated Queen
When you look in the mirror, what do you see?
Is it royalty?
Is it the vision of your unmatched beauty?
I see you do you see me?
We are the mothers of the earth
Seeds planted by our kings nurture our very nature
in which life does emerge
Submerge yourself in the wave of your beauty
So many imitate you and me
Melanated Queen
When you look in the mirror, what do you see?
Is it love unapologetically?
Is it the realization that you are unique?
I see you do you see me?
From your crown to your feet
And the frequency that vibes in between
Goddess love, you are the epitome
When you look in the mirror, do you see
You're a Melanated Queen.

Remember who you are in every step of your journey. You are worthy of all the beautiful blessings coming your way. Love always, Jess"

Niecy turned and hugged Jess.

"You haven't even opened the present yet," Jess laughed.

"You know yo' poetry is always enough for me. Yo' pen game is *crazy*," Niecy smiled.

"Thank you, but this ain't' about me right now," Jess smiled.

Niecy opened the small box and her eyes filled with tears. She turned to Jess and hugged her.

"Well?" Mahogany said after a moment, "What is it?"

Niecy released Jess and pulled out the contents of the box.

"A ticket to go see my dad."

The ladies smiled.

"It's actually a little bit more than that. I've been talking to Clarence more than you know. We talk a lot about his case.." she smiled brightly as she paused a moment.

Niecy's eyes squinted. It was easy to see she knew where this was going but didn't want to anticipate such a hopeful moment.

Jess continued, "Since marijuana is legal in Arizona now and he's already served the majority of his sentence-"

"Which we know was overkill in the first place," Mama Copeland cut in.

"Facts," Jess said before she continued, "They're letting him out early. That ticket is so you can be there when they do."

"We have the shop covered so you can take whatever time you need, dear," Mama Copeland said.

Niecy couldn't hold back any longer. Her eyes filled with tears, and they fell as she hugged Jess again.

"He reached out to us because he didn't want to get your hopes up and something happen, but it's official! He's coming home!" Jess said as she embraced her lil' sis'.

The room filled with laughter, smiles, and lots of tears. Niecy felt lucky, blessed, and grateful to have this, her family. The afternoon carried on with food and love until Niecy noticed the time.

"It's midnight ya'll!" Niecy said, looking at her phone.

"Happy birthday for real for real now," Jess said loudly.

"Happy birthday," Mahogany and Mama Copeland echoed in unison.

It was "turn twenty-one and drink until you can't remember, but you know you had a good night", time. Jess, Niecy, and Mahogany each gave Mama Copeland a hug and loving kiss on the cheek then left for their night out.

It was only a ten-minute drive to the bar in the heart of downtown. They were barely parked when Niecy jumped out and began twerking to the loud music coming from a passing car. She was clearly ready to have a good time.

"It's my biiirthdaaaay!" Niecy yelled in excitement.

A passing car honked as it's passengers yelled, "Happy biiirthdaaaay!"

Jess and Mahogany jumped out of the car quickly to catch up. As they walked into the bar, Jess felt her breath catch.

She spotted him before he spotted her, but as if he could feel her energy, he turned, and they locked eyes.

He smiled and mouthed, "Long Island."

Chapter Nine
No Barz

"Funny running into you here," Mahogany said with a giggle as they walked to the bar. She glanced at Jess.

They'd come to celebrate Niecy's birthday, and out of all the places they could choose, they ended up at the one with Rashawn behind the bar. Jess was happy to see him, but that was the problem. She saw him mouth the words "Long Island" and her heart skipped a beat. He had an effect on her that she wasn't sure she was ready for.

"This is Niecy," Jess said quickly to avoid the awkward moment Mahogany was creating with a grin, "She's twenty-one today."

"Happy birthday," Rashawn said, "Do you have something in mind or can I surprise you?"

"Surprise me!"

Rashawn smiled and then walked away to make the drinks.

"He's *cute*," Niecy said to Jess, "That's your new friend?"

"Yup," Mahogany interjected loudly.

Jess rolled her eyes. She caught a glimpse of Rashawn as he grinned, no doubt hearing the comment.

"Ya'll are childish," Jess said with a laugh.

Rashawn walked back over with three drinks and three shots.

"Birthday shots on me," Rashawn said, holding up a fourth shot glass. The ladies joined his drink in the sky.

"To Niecy," Rashawn said, "You made another rotation and are blessed to start a new year of life. Enjoy every second of it, starting right now!"

They touched glasses and took a gulp of the strong rum. Niecy followed by biting into a sliced lemon as she squinted her eyes.

"Niecy!" A voice came from behind. The ladies were soon in the company of several of Niecy's friends who quickly escorted her to the dance floor. Mahogany started moving to the music and followed, leaving Jess with Rashawn.

She looked on at the group having fun and smiled.

"So you know you could've just called," Rashawn said with a grin, "You didn't have to find a way to see me."

"Boy please," Jess rolled her eyes playfully, "I didn't even choose this place."

"Oh, so it was destiny. Stars aligning and all that?"

Jess's smile was interrupted by another patron waving his hand to get Rashawn's attention. She watched as he tended to the customer. He seemed to be moving in slow motion as he mixed the drink. How she had never truly taken in how sexy he was all this time made Jess shake her head.

"I did call you though," Rashawn said as he walked back over to Jess.

"My bad," she responded, "I was trying to get a special gift together for Niecy and forgot to call you back."

That was only partially true. After their perfect date, Jess found her mind drifting to him every chance it got. That night she'd tried to distract herself by calling Marcus, but that didn't work because every touch she imagined was from Rashawn.

Though she was willing to keep her life moving, she had to acknowledge that her feelings were moving faster than her intentions. She didn't want to end up falling too fast. Her previous relationship with Erick was still fresh, as toxic as it may have been. Her feelings for him were quickly disappearing from her heart, but that didn't mean it was time to jump head-first into something else.

"I get it," Rashawn broke through her thoughts, "you'll call when you're ready. I'm a patient man."

Jess smiled again.

"Just don't be stalking me at my jobs," he said with another playful grin.

Mahogany walked to the bar and grabbed Jess by the shoulder.

"Come to the bathroom with me," she said just loud enough for Jess to hear.

Jess pushed her now empty glass toward Rashawn and signaled she would return. She followed her friend's quick pace to the ladies' room in the back.

"Girl, what's wrong with you?" Jess asked in confusion as they allowed the door to close behind them.

"Erick is here," Mahogany said.

"Are you serious?" Jess's voice expressed pure annoyance.

She didn't want this night ruined but based on their last encounter, she had little faith that anything good could come of this.

"Yeah, he walked in, but I grabbed you before he saw you."

"The last time I saw him was not good," Jess said.

"I know," Mahogany paused a moment, "I saw you vibing with Rashawn and I just wanted to at least give you a head's up."

"It really shouldn't matter who I'm vibin' with," Jess responded defiantly.

"I know that and you know that, but you know niggas g'on nig every chance they get," Mahogany replied.

"Well I'm just going to ignore him. Hopefully he'll ignore me. I'm here to enjoy Niecy's night and I'm not about to be hiding in the bathroom."

With that, Jess turned and headed back out to the bar with Mahogany behind her. She returned to her bar seat, not even attempting to locate Erick. She hoped if she didn't look for him, maybe he wouldn't find her.

"Can we get another shot?," Jess said to Rashawn as she tried to ignore her pounding heart.

Now it was beating for two reasons. On the one hand, the very presence of Rashawn brought on a passionate pounding, and butterflies filled her belly. On the other, a stabbing sensation pierced through the passion and squeezed the life from each butterfly that fluttered inside from the very thought of another encounter with a man she'd once hoped she'd spend forever with.

Their shots were poured and consumed quickly. All Jess wanted to do in the moment was relax. She exhaled slowly as she felt the liquid enter her bloodstream and warm her body. What she wouldn't do for a fat blunt right then. Unfortunately, local laws didn't allow for smoking marijuana yet. She could hardly wait for that day, but today just wasn't it.

"You good?" Rashawn asked Jess.

"Yeah, you good?" Erick's voice rang behind her.

Jess looked at Mahogany, and they both rolled their eyes.

She looked at Rashawn, "I'm good."

"Oh, so we're ignoring now," Erick said, walking to her side.

Rashawn looked at Jess for confirmation that she was, in fact, good. Mahogany caught his attention and nodded an affirmative "*she got this*".

Jess turned to Erick, "The last time I talked to you about time and place, you let me know how you felt. So now you can leave me alone to wonder why I'm single," she said, recalling his last words to her.

"You know I was just mad," Erick replied with a smile that used to melt her heart. It only disgusted her in that moment.

How did she not see through it before? His arrogance seemed to be screaming at her now. Jess shook her head in disbelief. He really thought a smile would do it.

"I'm here celebrating a birthday," Jess said, "I'm not doing this with you right now."

Jess could see Rashawn glance down at her from the other end of the bar where he was serving another customer.

"Aht! Aht!," Niecy's loud drunk voice came from behind, "Not tonight! Ya'll not finna mess up my night. Go home to yo' baby mama!"

"Seriously, Erick," Mahogany cut in before Niecy could continue. Who knows what would come out of her mouth next.

Jess jumped in, "You said what you had to say. Leave it alone."

Erick looked like he was about to speak, then stopped. He looked at Jess again and walked away.

As he left, Jess felt proud of herself for keeping her cool. When she heard his voice, a flood of emotions went over her. It was mostly an annoyance, but him being able to evoke any emotion made her wonder how much more healing she needed.

"Are you okay?" Mahogany asked.

"Yeah, I'll be fine," she looked at Niecy, "Sorry girl. Let's go dance this negativity off."

Jess and Mahogany followed Niecy back to the dancefloor. As the night went on, Jess glanced toward Rashawn. She'd smile, and he'd nod. A drink was waiting each time she got to the bar. Mahogany would have to be the designated driver tonight. She needed to escape the confusion in her mind. Not even a line of poetry could creep in.

Jess allowed the drinks to flow and the vibes to emanate until she was lost in the night. At the end of the night she left without saying goodbye to Rashawn. The humiliation of it all was too much to deal with in the moment. She'd figure out her feelings tomorrow.

Chapter Ten
Eternity

Jess hesitated before she answered the phone.

"I'm so sorry I left like that," she said to Rashawn, skipping a greeting.

"It's cool," he replied, "I'm just checking on you. You looked like you had a lot going on."

Jess could feel a surge of embarrassment run through her body.

"Yeah, that was a lot."

"The ex?" Rashawn asked.

"Yup," was her empty reply.

Jess had no interest in getting into a deep conversation about Erick. She liked Rashawn…a lot, and the last thing she needed was to mess up something that could be good over something clearly bad.

"How are you?"

"I'm okay. It was more of a shock and annoyance at myself for even allowing him to upset me."

Jess felt comfortable talking to Rashawn. Even though her mind told her to keep her mouth closed, his energy just pulled out everything she tried to hold in. She felt herself relax hearing his voice.

"It's natural," he said, "it's still fresh. You don't gotta want to be with him for you to still have an emotional response."

Jess felt her heart pull closer to him with his understanding words. She needed to hear someone else tell her she wasn't trippin'. She didn't want to be with Erick. As a matter of fact, everything she'd learned about him disgusted her. Even with that though, she felt a twist in her stomach when she heard his voice. She could never love him again, he wasn't a factor, but she'd spent the night beating herself up for allowing him to work her nerves the way he had.

For some reason Jess had gotten it in her mind that not loving Erick meant being immune to any emotion that any other human being in her position would have felt. But hearing Rashawn's understanding words set her mind at ease. He understood her.

When had he even gotten the chance to learn her so well? Was it just as effortless for him as it was for her?

"I appreciate you," Jess heard herself say.

"Look," Rashawn said gently, "I'm not going to downplay my feelings. I like you. You have a vibe I really rock with."

Jess waited for the "but".

It didn't come.

"I'm letting you know I see you. I'm a patient man and I'll be here as your friend until you're ready for more."

Jess exhaled slowly and let his words wrap around her like a warm blanket. It didn't take a long conversation or lengthy proclamations. He knew what to say and how to say it. She felt every bit of it. In that moment, she could feel a few bricks being chipped away at the wall surrounding her heart.

"Thank you," she said softly.

"Well, I know you got shit to do so enjoy your day. Make it as beautiful as your spirit," he said, his voice smooth like butter.

Jess's smile matched what she imagined his was, "Thanks for checking on me."

"Fa sho," he responded.

"Make it as beautiful as your spirit" rang in Jess's head as she ended the call. That man knew how to strum at her heart strings. He seemed to always know exactly what to say.

Jess's phone vibrated in her hand as a text came through. A video clip from Rashawn. Curious, she pressed play.

Rashawn sat in a dark room with nothing but the flickering of a candle and the essence of smoke in the air.

"I'm working on something," he said into the camera, "Tell me what you think." With that, he cleared his throat and began,

"If the plan is for forever,
then the wait right now is of no consequence
Your essence exudes confidence
Your beauty is constant and
I just enjoy being in the energy of you," he paused, inhaling gently before he continued.
"So I'll give you time to release the weight from
past instances and remain consistent in
My support of you
I can wait for that smile to be for me
Cuz when you smile for anything, it brings me peace
The calm of a beautiful sea
I want you to know I see you, Queen
And I'm waiting patiently
For the day when I can fill your love with my space
Wait
I know that innuendo was evident, but it wasn't
my full intent
Only part of it
I know you're smiling a bit."

Jess shook her head with a grin. Yeah, she was smiling...more than a bit.

"And that's all I really want if I'm to be honest
A foundation that is solid
Love and laughter cuz that toxic shit ain't it
We can start forever now or wait
Cuz there's no such thing as too late
When viewing time in relativity
And you understand each moment is eternity."

Jess hadn't stopped smiling. She had no idea that Rashawn was a poet. She'd been going to Verse One for years and never witnessed him recite anything.

That was super dope. I really loved it, she typed in response with a heart eye emoji.

She wanted to type more, but the subject hadn't escaped her notice. It made her feel so good to know that he was feeling this way, but with all the chaos in her mind, she really didn't know how to respond.

He could see she needed time, and his noticing drew her closer to him. At the same time, she still faced the ongoing battle of trying to do things right. She was tired of relationships that didn't work. Yeah, she could be happy alone, but did she want that?

Simply put…NO! Many people don't understand that just because a woman says she can do life on her own doesn't mean she wants to. Like seriously, how did men expect them to survive until one of them came along as the provider they claimed to want to be? Was she supposed to never get her oil changed or take out her trash? Women like her just had to figure life out until someone came along that could relieve those burdens from her. And Jess would gladly relieve them! She was truly tired of doing it on her own. She wanted her next time to be her last time.

Glad you loved it. Have a good day, beautiful.

Jess replied by Loving the message. She really could see herself falling for this man. She felt herself wishing she could fast forward through her healing, but even Rashawn recognized that wasn't a healthy option.

She smiled again as she replayed the video. She would have a day as beautiful as her spirit because in this one video

Rashawn had brightened any darkness that had lingered from her encounter with Erick. And that's all she needed.

Chapter Eleven
The Other Side of Pain

"Damn, Jess," Mahogany said with a laugh, "You got this man writing poetry?"

Jess playfully snatched her phone from Mahogany's hand. The smile from Rashawn's poem remained on her face through the evening, straight to the morning breakfast she enjoyed with her best friend.

"Did you know he writes?" Jess asked.

"Nope. All these years that man's been working the bar at Verse One and not once have I seen him even watch an artist with interest. This caught me off guard in the greatest way," Mahogany replied.

"Yeah, it's a nice surprise," Jess smiled.

Mahogany took a sip of her coffee from the oversized steamed mug, "I know I keep telling you to be careful, but I've *never* seen you smile like that."

"So I *shouldn't* be careful," Jess said mischievously.

Mahogany rolled her eyes in jest, "Girl, you know what I'm saying."

"Yeah," Jess could feel her ears heat up with her black girl blush.

"Take your time but move forward if you think you're ready. There's no fixed timeline on your healing journey."

Jess sighed.

"What's on your mind?" Mahogany asked.

"I'mma have to cut Marcus off ain't I?"

Mahogany burst into a hard laugh, "Girl!"

"The sex is so good though," Jess poked out her bottom lip childishly.

"Well, it's not like you're getting married tomorrow. I say keep him around until you and Rashawn are locked in. The last thing you want to do is waste some good *D* on a *maybe*," Mahogany said, ending with a slight rhythm.

"Barz!" Jess replied, giggling.

"I told you I got a couple of rhymes in me," Mahogany laughed then drifted off in thought.

"And what's on *your* mind?" Jess asked.

"Did I tell you Marcus is Tavis's son's name too?"

"You miss him don't you?"

"Every day," Mahogany smiled.

Jess could only imagine finding a love so pure and intentional as the one Mahogany found in Jamaica. They understood that their romance was only for the island, but to Jess it didn't seem fair. Mahogany's heart was so untainted and she deserved to have someone that made her smile the way the memory of Tavis did weeks after they separated. Was it really better to have loved and lost? Wasn't the memory torturous at times?

"I don't know how you do it," Jess said sighing, "I would've gotten his number just in case."

Mahogany laughed lightly, "Don't think I didn't consider it."

"What stopped you?"

"My purpose," Mahogany stood and walked to the sink with her now empty coffee mug, "I didn't go down there for that. I went to find a muse. I found one. It was beautiful. *He* was beautiful. And with that, I have a beautifully untainted memory that can be the muse for so much more."

Jess admired her friend. As Mahogany walked back to her seat Jess noticed the sun compliment her melanated skin. She really was stunning, but it was more than that. The rays of the sun seem to bring out the beauty of Mahogany's spirit as well.

"I pray that your experience was only a glimpse of the lifetime of love you will have."

"Awe, *friend*," Mahogany touched the top of Jess's hand.

"I really do mean it," Jess said as she placed her free hand on top of Mahogany's.

The ladies sat in silence, each submerged in imaginings of what they hoped their futures would bring.

"So you had your date, you even got a poem out of it," Mahogany said, breaking the silence, "Would you say you're over Erick now?"

"To be honest," Jess began, "Now that I look back I don't think I was ever *under* him," she laughed.

Mahogany joined, "Funny enough, I know you well enough to know exactly what you mean."

"Right, like I don't know what I was even thinking," Jess paused a moment then continued, "This has nothing to do with Rashawn, but I really feel like I had to be insane to stay blind to who Erick was showing me. Even without this new thing starting I would be fine."

"And the way he was acting up at Niecy's birthday…" Mahogany let her voice trail off.

"Girl, that was so embarrassing. I was sitting there the whole time trying to figure out what the hell I ever saw in him. Like, did he change?"

"No!" Mahogany said almost too loudly.

Jess's eyes widened at her friend's bold reaction.

Mahogany continued, "Listen, I won't lie, I hated how everything happened, but I was glad you saw him for who he truly is before you got too deep. Someone can be okay in many ways, but that doesn't make them okay for you. You know I know this from experience."

Jess nodded her head. Mahogany almost married a man she didn't love. No, he didn't cheat like Erick did, but still, he wasn't the right fit. Jess saw it and only hoped it would work itself out. It did, but not in the way anyone expected. Mahogany walked away shortly before their wedding day. She didn't want to feel trapped. Jess couldn't help but wonder if that is how she would have felt had she stayed with Erick.

"Hindsight is twenty-twenty," Jess said.

"Clear as an Arizona sky," Mahogany replied.

"Honestly, I just feel more at peace. I still have some work to do and I don't want Rashawn to be a band-aid. He is more than that."

Mahogany nodded, "I get that. That's why I say keep Marcus around."

Jess laughed, "Yeah, if for no other reason than to keep my emotions at bay with Rashawn."

"My mother would kill me if she heard me giving you this advice," Mahogany said laughing.

Jess joined, "Girl, mine would call on all the ancestors if she knew I agreed."

"But times change and so do these men. You gotta act accordingly."

"Absolute facts," Jess said still laughing.

Jess picked up her phone and opened her Notes app as a thought came to her mind.

It feels so good on the other side of pain
And thoughts of him are no longer main
Not even secondary it's almost as if they never existed
And I won't lie my heart fought hard to resist it
But when I imagined a new kiss on my lips
I knew he and I could never again be
Not that the new kiss wiped away the old
It just revealed there is a new story that needs to be told
About me and the aftermath

"Girl!" Mahogany said loudly, breaking Jess's flow.

"What?" Jess knew it had to be important. Mahogany was used to Jess going into one of her writer dazes at any moment and she usually didn't disrupt that.

Mahogany turned her phone to Jess. Her mouth dropped for a moment then turned into a smile.

"Looks like someone wants more than a memory," Jess said as she looked at the notification on Mahogany's phone.

She'd posted about finding a muse in Jamaica and that her followers should be ready for her best work yet.

Her post gained a new Heart response.

"Tavis," Mahogany almost whispered.

Chapter Twelve
Soul's Mate

"Tap on his profile and let me see what he looks like," Jess said with a curious grin.

"I can't believe he looked for me," Mahogany said as she pulled up his profile.

Jess looked on as her friend landed on a picture of Tavis. Her eyes locked on and Jess could only imagine the emotions that flooded Mahogany's heart in that moment.

"You okay, luv?"

"I didn't realize how much I missed him," Mahogany said as she handed Jess her phone.

Jess looked at the wedding picture in Jamaica. Tavis was the Best Man, and she could see why her friend had so effortlessly fallen in love in a week.

"Damn, he's fine as hell," Jess said as she began to scroll through his other pictures.

She handed Mahogany back the phone, "I thought your page was private though."

Mahogany looked down embarrassingly.

"Girl," Jess said laughing, "You made your page public so he could see you. You ain't slick."

Mahogany looked up and put her palm to her face, "Yeah," she laughed shyly, "Girl, I didn't think he'd actually find me though. He has a lot going on."

"Yeah, but ya'll had something special. You don't just forget that."

"I never want to forget."

"So what is it?"

"I don't want that feeling to ever be tainted," Mahogany stared off in a distance, "I want what we had to be my piece of perfection forever."

They allowed the sentiment to float through the air.

Jess could only imagine what that type of love felt like. She understood her friend. In every relationship there are ups and downs. Once the downs appear they can't be completely erased. Having a clear understanding when Mahogany and Tavis parted ways was a perfect ending to a love that would be everlasting in their hearts. Jess only wondered if her friend not taking a chance would leave her without ever exploring the possibilities of her true soul's mate.

"So, what are you going to do, friend?" Jess asked gently.

Mahogany shrugged, "I honestly don't know."

"Well, you don't have to know right now. Just make sure that you don't allow fear to decide for you."

Mahogany turned and looked at her friend. Scratch that, her *sister*. No one else knew her inside and out better than the woman who sat before her.

Jess smiled and stood then walked to the bathroom, "You wanna come to Verse One tonight?"

"Nah, I'm going to head home in a little bit," Mahogany called out as Jess went into the bathroom, "My mother is really on me about this exhibit."

Jess stuck her head out the doorway and smiled at Mahogany.

"Daaang! All he did was Like a post and you over there inspired," Jess giggled as her head disappeared back into the bathroom.

"Didn't that post say that man was my muse," Mahogany replied sharing Jess's giggle.

Jess stared at her reflection in the mirror as she thought about Rashawn. She turned on the faucet to begin her beauty routine and found herself lost in the water.

I wonder if I'll ever have that.

"Besides," Mahogany said from the kitchen, "You have Rashawn there to keep you company."

Jess's eyes broke from the water as she smiled.

"I can hear your smile from in here," Mahogany called out.

"Now explain to me how you hear a smile," Jess responded as she began to wash her face.

"Was I right?"

"Yeah."

"Okay then," Mahogany laughed, "Don't question my wisdom."

Jess rinsed off her face and stuck her head out the doorway again.

"You sound like my mother."

"Thank you," Mahogany responded as Jess rolled her eyes.

Mahogany got up and gathered her things. Jess was standing in the mirror moisturizing her face when Mahogany appeared beside her.

"I'll keep an open mind about Tavis," Mahogany continued, breaking the quick smile on Jess's face, "That's only *if* he even reaches out."

"That's fair," Jess said.

"In the meantime, you, my good sis, keep an open mind with Rashawn," Mahogany said, "Ya'll have good energy. If you think you're ready I think you should explore it."

Jess nodded in agreement. She turned and hugged her friend.

"Use your key to lock up for me please," Jess said as she turned back to the mirror.

"Gotchu," Mahogany said as she left.

Jess's mind filled with thoughts and emotions as she applied her makeup and styled her hair. She wanted love. She was ready. Her past had taken up too much of her energy and she wanted to be able to have the life she deserved. Fear was a major part of her hesitance, but she couldn't advise Mahogany to follow her heart and then turn and do the opposite.

Jess really like Rashawn. There was nothing not to like. He seemed to be different from men she'd dated in the past, which was a good thing. A refreshing break from the same type of men that seemed to creep into her life.

"Flow with it girl," Jess said as she looked in her full-length mirror, "Stop overthinking. Listen and hear how you're being guided. You're worth it."

She smiled as she left to head to Verse One.

*****

"Sometimes you don't get to be with your soul's mate
Instead when your souls mate it aids in your growth
to be prepared for your life mate
And the two can equate with life exceeding
The former meaning of the one you thought
your soul would forever be tied to
And perhaps it is

> Soul ties are not easily broken especially when
> woven with threads of love
> So you learn from what was to create what will be
> And permit yourself to be happy
> Joy exceeding love completing
> Souls mating…"

Jess snapped her fingers in approval as she listened to the beautiful poet who took to the stage at Verse One. She turned and glanced back at Rashawn and they locked eyes. He gave her a quick wink before turning his attention to a patron to take their order.

Have I ever even really had a soulmate? Jess wondered. She'd dated and felt energies before, but she desired to be with someone who made her spine tingle at the thought of him. Someone who would make her soul dance at the memory of his touch. Had she ever really experienced that?

She didn't know the answer to the past, but in the present, she felt it. A shiver ran through her body when Rashawn locked eyes with her a moment before. In that span of a millisecond, she imagined his lips on hers. His touch on hers. And though the sexuality of that was good, it wasn't at the forefront of her mind. The intimacy. In one look the room seemed to empty and they stared at each other alone.

> "Sometimes, if blessed, you do get to be with your
> soul's mate
> So when your souls mate the rhythm makes your
> souls quake
> In sync
> So the future meaning of your love is ever present
> in the past recognition of who you are to be
> To each other

Father, mother as you birth peace and love for
those within your radius
Intertwining your souls with purpose
And when you and your soulmate allow your
souls to mate
You feel the energy of the proximity of your soul's mate
The passion behind those "only you" eyes
Now, babaaay, that's a soul tie…"

The artist continued but once again the room emptied as Jess turned, this time catching Rashawn already staring at her. The look he gave felt like the "only you" look that was described in the piece that had seemed to be speaking to them both. The same chill that ran through the body the first time they locked eyes made an encore appearance.

"Nightcap?," she saw Rashawn mouth to her.

Jess smiled and nodded. Something was in the air and she had wondered if he felt it too. His invitation meant he had and Jess could feel her heart speed up.

Jess's phone lit up as a text alert appeared on her screen. She looked down and frowned.

Slide through later?

Only hours before the thought of cutting Marcus off seemed unreasonable. As Jess responded, *Not tonight,* she felt like that time might be coming sooner than she thought.

She had a feeling she'd know for sure after her nightcap.

Chapter Thirteen
Nightcap

"Yeah, I believe in soulmates," Jess responded to Rashawn with a smile.

Normally Jess loved every moment of Verse One, but after Rashawn had asked her for a nightcap the time seemed to slow to a snail's pace. She wanted to be alone with him and the clock just wouldn't cooperate.

But here they were. In the parking lot passing a marijuana blunt in Rashawn's darkly tinted SUV. The conversation quickly turned to matters of the heart and surprisingly to Jess, it didn't scare her. His conversation only stimulated her more, but she would be patient and allow him to lead. Something else new to her.

"Growing up there was more focus on staying away from soul ties, instead of looking for soulmates," Rashawn shook his head.

Jess took that statement in for a moment.

"So be for real with me."

"Of course."

"What are you ready for? I mean," Jess thought of her next words, "I'm not trying to lock you down right now, but the energy is clearly there. I don't want to guess."

Rashawn paused in thought.

"Was that too much?" Jess asked.

"Nah," Rashawn answered, "You're good."

They sat for a moment more, "I meant it when I said I'm not out here like that. I'm ready to relax and chill," Rashawn inhaled the marijuana before continuing, "I'm not going to say I know you're my soulmate, but I wanna take some time to find out."

Jess could feel that chill run up her spine. Before the sensation could come to completion she shook her head to bring her back to the moment. She took the tightly rolled leaf blunt and held it between her thumb and first finger. She stared at it, then at him. She smiled, inhaled, and moved closer to his face.

Rashawn leaned in and allowed the smoke Jess exhaled to enter his system as he gently grabbed her chin. She felt a rush as he pulled her face closer to his, slowly filling the space the smoke once held with their lips.

A rush came over her as Jess's body reacted to this gentle kiss that held a passion she'd never felt before. There was absolutely no doubt in her mind he felt it too. This type of energy was more than one person could consume so it had to be shared.

Their lips parted.

"Nightcap?" Rashawn said.

"Nightcap," Jess confirmed.

Jess had taken a rideshare to Verse One because she'd decided tonight would be a drinking night. She ended up only having one drink but the entire ride to Rashawn's house she'd felt an intoxication fill her body. It wasn't nerves, it wasn't excitement. It was more of...an anticipation.

As they rode along I-75 South Rashawn kept the conversation flowing, allowing their frequencies to completely sync. She could tell he understood what was needed. However, an oral precursor to what was to come was unneeded. Unwanted. This casual conversation was perfect.

As they pulled into Rashawn's neighborhood he turned down the late-night 90s R&B sounds that had played background to the ride. He turned left, sighed, and turned right. Rashawn turned the music completely silent and Jess felt him squeeze her hand.

Until that moment Jess had not even realized they were already holding hands. The question of when they'd started creeped in when blue and red lights began to flash in the rearview mirror. Jess turned and glanced at Rashawn. A mixture of fear, frustration, and anger filled his eyes. He glanced at Jess and then pulled the car over to the left. As he came to a stop, Rashawn grabbed his license and registration from the open console under his radio. Jess instinctively reached up and turned on the lights inside the vehicle.

The police car's bright flood light consumed the car as his shadowy figure exited and walked to the driver's side.

"License and registration," the officer said as he approached Rashawn's window.

Rashawn handed the requested information and Jess noticed the officer's light beige hand reach for the documents while the other rested on his firearm that sat in its unlatched holster.

Rashawn placed his hands on the steering wheel and gripped it firmly.

"Hold tight," the officer said then walked back to his car.

"Why didn't you ask him why he pulled you over?" Jess asked quietly.

"Because I already know," he responded shortly.

Jess stared at Rashawn for a moment before turning her focus forward. Her heart quickened as the officer returned to the driver's side window.

"Do you know why I pulled you over?"

Rashawn gripped the wheel tighter, "We *both* know why you pulled me over."

The officer tensed up and clenched his jaws, "You didn't come to a complete stop back there."

"So your hand's on your gun cuz of a rolling stop?" Jess said, annoyed.

Rashawn snapped his head toward her, "*Chill.*"

Frustrated, Jess retreated in her seat.

The officer sighed, his hand still resting on his gun, "I'm going to do you a favor and just give you a warning."

Jess huffed. Rashawn gripped the wheel again. She silenced herself.

The officer handed Rashawn's license and registration back, along with a white paper. He took the stack, placed them back in the open console, and gripped the wheel once again. Jess could see his jaw tighten and loosen over and over.

"Get home safe, now," the officer said nonchalantly, tapping the hood as he walked back to his car and turned off the lights.

Only then did Jess notice the many window blinds that were open in the houses around them.

Rashawn waited for the officer to make a U-turn and drive away before he headed three houses down from where they were stopped and turned into the driveway.

"I didn't mean to snap at you," he said, finally loosening his grip on the wheel.

"I get it," she responded.

"I almost wish I never bought this house," he said, "You'd think I was living in a million-dollar mansion-"

"But it's like we're not allowed to live anywhere outside the 'hood, no matter what level," Jess added.

"Exactly."

Rashawn turned the car off and exhaled deeply.

"If I come home at night, I'm damn near guaranteed to get pulled over," Rashawn breathed deeply.

Jess could see not only frustration, but sadness. This had to happen often because Rashawn was a bartender. He was bound to leave wherever he was late at night and even early morning. Her heart sank imagining the type of anxiety that routine could create.

"One of the most heartbreaking things is to love a country that refuses to love you back," she said softly.

Rashawn looked over at Jess and for a moment they locked eyes. The energy that was exchanged between them held no need for words. It was understood that no matter how hard they worked some melanin-deficient folks would only see them as intruders on an already stolen land...but those same people would never admit that last part.

"Nightcap" seemed to hold a new meaning.

When the bullshit becomes an acceptable
expectation that's when we have problems
So...how do we solve them?
We yell and scream then gasp for air as we protest and
it falls on deaf ears
Do you even care?
Clearly not
Do you know what it is to have a panic attack at
even the chance of a traffic stop by the cop that just
"happened to pull up behind you"?
Now mind you...you're riding squeaky clean
But what does that really mean?

So…boom….panic attack
But not just any panic attack…no
This one you have to internalize as you feel
the burn in your eyes
And the tightness in your chest
Your body takes you on a quest
Your breath wants to quicken but you can't
reveal that your deep fears are attacking your mind…
you must conceal
That you're in a state of panic
Before you can think about it
Your brain sends random signals of pain to your body
You pray "Please don't notice me"
Do you know what that feels like?
To live in a world where living while black might
cost you your life?
Headed home for a nightcap only to end up
capped cuz you're black
By this nation's knight in blue equipped with Kevlar
armor
And even though you're unarmed
They still claim they feared for their life so they
shot cuz they couldn't disarm or
Defuse the situation
Smiling in elation cuz they know we'll never
get our reparations
And therefore never be placed on equal grounds
Instead forced to lay on the ground
Hands behind the head, legged crossed
All we see is a burning cross in their eyes
No lies are being told when we wonder if we'll
ever get to grow old
All because we are driving home for a nightcap
Think about that

Chapter Fourteen
Follow The Leader/Encore

For many people in the U.S., a "simple traffic stop" that didn't end in a ticket would be a situation that would quickly be turned into a memory as life moves forward. However, for a Black man in this country those situations, especially when done so often, can leave him in a state of fear, frustration, helplessness, and even anger. The P.T.S.D. that this land of the free has brought on Black folks is often a subject dismissed and ignored.

So in that moment, sex was the last thing on Jess's mind. All she wanted was to give Rashawn a safe space to be as vulnerable as he needed. It was evident that this was not a one-off. An instance that could be chalked up as a grumpy cop. From Jess's understanding, this happened weekly. WEEKLY!

Rashawn's mood was a bit lighter as he tried to provide a cool vibe for Jess. As aggravating as it was, what happened earlier was over. He did not want to make the night worse by dwelling on it. He'd been patient as he watched her every movement whenever they shared a space. He was a gentleman, of course, but tonight was when he wanted to show her that he could be a gentle man for her.

The almost routine encounter seemed to get under Rashawn's skin more than he intended. He knew a part of it was the embarrassment of this happening in front of Jess. He didn't like the idea of her seeing him in any sort of criminal light. He'd never been in trouble with the law and prided himself on that fact.

Jess sat on his couch next to him, her hand gently rubbing Rashawn's back as if this was something they did regularly. She paused momentarily to take a sip of the drink he'd made for her, but as she placed the glass back down her hand continued to touch him, not losing the rhythm his heart had fallen in sync with. They fit so well that even in a moment like this she knew what he needed and acted, unprompted.

Rashawn began rolling a marijuana joint, relaxing his tension with each gentle stroke of her fingernails. Up. Down. A smooth rhythm that removed his embarrassment and frustration. He wanted to return to the place they were before the red and blue lights flashed behind them. The event seemed to be pushed further to the back of his mind and his breathing slowed to an even inhale, then exhale. She brought him a sense of peace, but not just from tonight's encounter. This type of peace rushed through his body. She was a comfort he didn't realize he needed.

Jess watched as Rashawn sealed the joint using his tongue and top lip to secure the closure. He lit it and began to smoke.

Jess continued rubbing his back as she traced his mouth with her eyes. Dear gawd this man was sexy. She felt him relax with each touch and as much as she tried to fight it, her body responded. As she felt his energy lighten her eyes began to rest on his every movement.

"So you gonna let me hit it?" Jess asked with a sly smile.

Rashawn turned his head with a grin and passed the joint. Jess took it and placed it between her lips as he watched. She inhaled deeply and held it. Then, turning to face him, Jess gently grabbed Rashawn's chin with her first finger and thumb. She pulled him close to her lips, almost touching, and released the smoke between them. He inhaled and he stared into her eyes.

The annoyance of the traffic stop was now in their rearview. As they looked ahead they had an unspoken understanding that they were back on course.

Rashawn leaned in to kiss Jess, but she smiled as she pulled back.

"I think you deserve to relax," Jess said softly gently pushing him back against the couch, "I got this."

Rashawn licked his lips as he looked at Jess, now standing in front of him. He stared as she slowly undressed, showing every part of her that had lived in his imagination. The reality was better than any dream.

She stepped in front of him and pulled his head to her sweetest spot. She felt the tongue that licked the joint lick her softly as his lips caressed every part it touched. Jess allowed this for only a moment, then pushed him back and slowly dropped to her knees.

Her thoughts drifted to the words that formed in her mind as she sat rubbing his back only moments before...and executed perfectly if she did say so herself.

Can you imagine all the passion that can happen if you just let me lead?

*Follow me to ecstasy and I'll lead you
through my fantasies
Shhhh...I ain't wearin' no panties
I've been yearning for you
Hot to the touch my heart is burning for you
I'm feeling urges for you
My mind is filled with lust it urgently needs you
Liquor used as fuel, you ignite what was only a flicker
As I move you down low for just a quick moment
to lick her
You don't have to do much...let your tongue touch
Just enough to tame your hunger
So now I can proceed to provide you with everything
you need
But never even realized
As I touch you and you look into my eyes
Unspoken lyrics lie between the lines
I'm oblivious to anything but us in this moment
Damn baby I really want it
Though you speak in a tenor a sonorous voice is heard
as your slightly warm breath tickles my nose
And causes chills to lead to the curling of my toes
This is only the beginning, our first time
When our souls tie*

They'd gone from the couch to the kitchen. There was a stop in the hallway as they couldn't wait for the few additional steps it would take to make it to his bed. But they eventually did. The bed cradled them as they moved in a rhythm, welcoming every movement and position. With each stroke they felt the cords of their souls intertwine until they were indistinguishable from each other.

They were connected and they knew in this moment that it was special. Something neither had felt before. There were no awkward moments. They moved as if they knew each other's bodies for a lifetime. As if this was an occasion they both celebrated, the explosion in their climaxes were the fireworks that rewarded them for a job well done. A mission accomplished.

Rashawn breathed deeply as he reminisced on moments before when Jess had taken charge and provided him with everything he desired. No one had ever been able to read him and please him the way this beautiful woman did.

He could see that her goal was to make their first night one they would never forget. She'd taken the situation into her own hands, leading him to ecstasy. She'd allowed him to bend her over the kitchen table as they headed to the bedroom taking control for a moment, but only for that moment, because tonight her objective was to please *him*.

The seduction between them as they traveled throughout his home, blessing every place, was everything they wanted it to be and more. When they were finished they relaxed into an embrace.

"You are so dope," Rashawn said and kissed the top of Jess's hair.

"I am, ain't I," Jess responded with a giggle.

"Yeah," Rashawn laughed, "you really are."

Jess turned further into his body as she took her fingers and began to trace from his chest to his navel. She stopped as she felt his stomach sink in with his sharp inhale. His reaction told a story of what their life could be in these moments.

Rashawn took her hand and held it in his for a moment. In one smooth movement, Jess found herself on her back as he held himself above her. He began to kiss her forehead, cheeks, nose, and finally her lips. She'd given herself a round of applause for her earlier performance, but he was clearly a part of the production and deserved his flowers. Jess relinquished control, handing the keys to this ride over to Rashawn. There was nothing better than an encore after a stellar performance.

You had rounds one, three and four
But now it's time I explore
Let me lay you on your back
As you relax
Enjoy me
Because your every inhale, moan, movement is
what I need
My mind has moved from the imaginations of the past
To the visions of the future, should we last
Everything in this moment tells me it will though
I kiss your lips up top before the ones below
The tremble in your thighs
As my tongue massages inside
Tasting like the river of life overflowing
And as if we've been here before I'm already knowing
What you require
What you desire
I provide it all with a gentle kiss here
Followed by a light touch there
I pull your hair as I give what you've been waiting for
The encore

Chapter Fifteen
Mahogany's Piece

"Can you *please* stop massaging me so hard," Niecy said lifting her head off the table, "I'm a lady. I don't like all that rough mess."

"*Niecy!*" Mahogany said in a joking reprimand. She lifted her head and turned to look at Niecy.

Niecy exchanged stares with Mahogany. The Black woman's conversation began in their eyes.

Niecy widened her eyes as if to say, *What?*

Mahogany tilted her head to the side and squinted saying, *Be nice.*

Niecy frowned and rolled her eyes, *Fine.*

"Thank you," Niecy threw back at the masseuse. She looked back at Mahogany and threw a sarcastic smile, *There! I was nice!*

Mahogany smiled and put her head back in the hole of her table. *That's better.*

"Sorry I'm late ya'll," Jess said as she walked into the massage room. She disrobed and laid on her stomach, "Make sure you don't massage too hard."

"Why did ya'll even come," Mahogany said laughing.

"What?" Jess asked.

"Nothing," Niecy responded.

"So," Mahogany said, "I stopped by last night and you weren't home."

"Oop," came Niecy's voice.

Mahogany continued, "I texted you and you ain't respond."

"Oop," repeated Niecy.

"I even called, but you ain't answer."

"This sounds like tea might be involved," Niecy chimed.

Jess let out an exaggerated exhale before she spoke, "I had my phone on Do Not Disturb," trying to sound nonchalant.

"Don't play with me," Mahogany said with a slight laugh.

"Fine," Jess smiled at the memories of the night before, "I was at Rashawn's house."

Niecy's head popped up, startling her masseuse, "That fine guy from my birthday?"

"Yup," Jess responded.

"Tell me everything," Mahogany said.

"We shouldn't even be doing all this talking," Jess said teasingly, "We're supposed to be relaxing."

"We're paying for this so we get to decide how to relax," Niecy said, "Now spill the tea!"

The ladies giggled as they settled into the semi-muffled story of the previous night. Jess had a rule never to give too many specifics on sex with a man she was involved with, but everything else was told in great detail.

Jess's story was ad-libbed with sounds of agreement and intrigue from Mahogany and Niecy as they sipped this proverbial tea their friend was serving piping hot. Even the three masseuses let out an occasional gasp as they listened on.

From the flirtations at the beginning to the police killing the mood in the middle to a rekindling of the previous romance at the end. Her retelling of her life was like watching a romantic movie from the 90's. The highs and lows while you hope for the happily ever after because the chemistry between the two main characters is beautiful and undeniable.

The story took the remaining time of their massage appointment so after their polite "thank yous" the additional ladies cleared the room.

"Girl," Mahogany started, "I know you got your rule and everything, but at least tell us on a scale of one to ten?"

Jess laughed, "I'll say this much...it was higher than a nine."

They all giggled like schoolgirls.

Mahogany sat up and wrapped her towel around her body, "Okay. So you got that out of your system, how do you feel?"

"Leave it to you to skip the sex to jump right to the emotions," Niecy said.

Jess laughed, "I feel fine," she paused a breath, "It was such a crazy night. One minute we're chillin' and enjoying the energy between us. Then that cop stopped us and everything just got tense. I honestly thought about leaving."

"I'm glad you didn't," Niecy said, "Men are sensitive and they get super emotional when they feel like you left them."

The ladies dressed as the conversation continued.

Mahogany let out a laugh and turned to Jess, "Remember when we switched for a day and I had to write a poem and you had to paint?"

Jess joined in the laughter at the memory, "Girl yes. I have no idea where that painting is, but I damn sure remember that poem."

Niecy's eyes widened, "Hold up," she grinned, "*Mahogany Waters* wrote a *poem*? Please tell me it didn't start with 'Roses are red and violets are blue'."

"No," Mahogany laughed, "It was better than that."

"Actually," Jess said, "It was pretty good."

"Do you remember it?" Niecy asked.

Mahogany cleared her throat,

"Niggaz is just like bitches
Yeah I said it
Niggaz is just like bitches
Now I'm not talking about real men and women
Kings and Queens
I'm talbout niggaz and bitches
Don't get it twisted
They wanna call their actions logic
But I call bullshit
They want what they want how they want it
And if you say no they can't handle it
They get all sensitive
Just like a bitch
Now I ain't no poet
But I call it how I see it
In whatever form it comes in…"

Niecy chuckled lightly. It was cute listening to this version of her sweet artistic friend.

Mahogany had a childish smile as she switched her cadence to that of a nursery rhyme,

"I'll say it loud
I'll say it proud
I'll say it to her and I'll say it to him
And if I don't know which one I'll say it to them
Your whining and complaining has me in stitches
Cuz I'm laughing at you niggaz that act like bitches."

Jess and Niecy snapped their fingers, the universal applause for spoken word audiences, and laughed.

"Okay," Niecy said, "I see you out here with a rhyme or two."

Mahogany took a playful bow, "I do what I can."

"It's funny, but it's so true," Jess said, "Men are way more sensitive than they let on."

"So yeah. I'm glad you didn't leave that man like that," Mahogany said, "I'd hate for him to ruin things before they really start."

Jess thought a moment, "I honestly don't think he's like that. He gives me real man energy," she paused, "King energy."

Both ladies gave Jess "the look" with raised eyebrows and pursed lips. Jess could feel her face warm as her vulnerability crept out.

"Ya'll hush."

"We didn't say anything," Niecy said, laughing.

"Not a word," Mahogany chimed in.

Neither had to say it. They saw it all over Jess's face. She was on a path to falling in love. They saw it and she felt it. As much as she thought it would be appropriate to take a step back and tame her desires, she also felt that she deserved to feel free. To be with a man that didn't send her guessing his every movement. A man who didn't cause doubt. She felt comfortable in his presence and safe in his arms. Rashawn could very well be the man she'd been writing about in her imaginative poems all these years. He could be the lyrics to her unwritten future.

Chapter Sixteen
Slow Journey To Love

Jess walked to the back of Motherland where she found her mother sitting with her feet up on an ottoman. Mama Copeland looked up and gave her daughter a light smile. Jess knew that look; her mother was tired.

"Awe, mama," Jess said walking over and leaning down for a hug and kiss on the cheek.

"I would say I don't look like what I've been through, but I have a feeling that wouldn't be true today," Mama Copeland replied.

"Nah, mama," Jess said sitting down in a chair next to her, "you're always beautiful no matter what's going on."

"Thank you, baby," Mama Copeland said.

"Was it busy today?"

"It was steady," Mama Copeland adjusted in her seat, "That's why I'm tired. I never got a chance to sit down. These kids learned what chakras are and now everyone wants to buy a crystal."

They laughed lightly.

"Well Motherland thanks them," Jess said, "Plus we can usually convince them to get a book to learn about what they're seeing on social media."

"And that makes it worth it," Mama Copeland replied.

Jess got up and walked to the counter and got a teacup.

"I forgot to tell you that someone came in asking for you today," Mama Copeland said to Jess.

She turned around with the teacup in one hand and the tea kettle in the other.

"Who?"

"I don't remember," she turned her head in thought, "I was helping out some ladies and they were asking a lot of questions. He asked for you, I said you weren't in, and he said thank you and left."

Jess wondered who would come to Motherland to look for her. Then decided she wasn't going to make a big mystery drama about it.

"They'll call me if they need me," Jess said shrugging her shoulders, "So are you going to close the store early to go to Mahogany's exhibit on Saturday?"

"I sure am," Mama Copeland said, her voice filled with pride, "She's finally doing it and I wouldn't miss it for the world."

"Yeah," Jess said and smiled, "I need a trip to Jamaica. Maybe I'll write an award-winning spoken word album. I just need a muse."

"It was more than just a trip," Mama Copeland said, "That girl came back with love written all over her energy."

"You felt it too?"

"How could I not?" Mama looked thoughtfully, "I just wish she hadn't run from it. I've never seen her aura so bright as when she got back."

"She didn't run, mama. They wanted to keep their perfect moment, perfect."

"It lost its perfection when they lost each other," Mama Copeland said, "her light isn't as bright as it was when she first got back."

She was right. Jess could see the longing in her friend's eyes every time she looked at her. Mahogany fell in love and she missed that feeling, but Jess didn't want to beat a dead horse. Her friend had told her she was happy with the memory of love and Jess had to accept it.

"Speaking of bright auras," Mama Copeland said as Jess returned to her seat.

"*What?*" Jess said as her mother stared at her.

"What's his name?"

Jess couldn't hide anything from her mother. She used to try and fight it, but that was long ago.

"Rashawn," she gave in with no fight.

"Is that the young man that came in here distracting you that day we were swamped?"

"Okay, mama," Jess laughed, "Do you remember the date and time too?"

"I know you'll formally introduce me when you're ready," Mama Copeland paused, "But are you sure you're ready for another relationship?"

Jess paused in thought. She felt the answer, but she knew her mother had a point. It wasn't long ago that she sat in this very room planning a seven day grieving period to move forward from the last relationship.

"That's a valid question," Jess paused a moment, "We care about each other a lot, but we want to take things slowly."

"And what does that mean?"

"It means I am not rushing to fall in love -"

"Love has no speed limit," Mama Copeland cut in.

Jess continued, "- and lose myself. I'm still healing and I know that, but I also know that he has a calming energy and we just make sense."

"Okay," there was a loud pause, "If you say you got this then I'll believe you. Just please be careful."

"I will, mama."

I'm patient
Because I've been waiting
And my heart won't take it
If it's taken advantage of again
I sometimes wondered when
It would truly happen for me
Now you're here and I pray you don't leave
You don't complete me
But our complete being in unity
Is a powerful force to be reckoned with
We are the shit
But we gotta be patient
Take time with it
My heart is delicate
Just because it heals doesn't mean there aren't scars
I see them as reminders that my love is large
It's just been given to those that misuse
But they are behind and my focus is on you
I see forever with you
So since it's forever we can take a breath or two
Before jumping in the end that's deep
You see
Forever begins now and lives for eternity
So let's take our slow journey to love patiently

Chapter Seventeen
Roadblocks

"So I'm going to leave after Mahogany's exhibit," Niecy said over the video call.

Jess closed the door behind her as she entered her apartment. She placed her bag down on her couch before responding.

"What time is your flight?" Jess asked.

"Like 6 in the morning. Arizona is 3 hours behind us so I'll get in early in the morning their time," Niecy replied. Her smile brightened her entire face.

Jess returned her smile, "I know you're so excited to see your dad."

Niecy nodded, "I swear I've been going to bed early all week trying to make this time go by."

"I'm really happy for you," Jess said, "We need our fathers."

"Thank you again," Niecy said, choking up a bit, "Like, we are family for life."

"Was that ever in question?" Jess said playfully. She took off her shoes and put them on the rack by the coat closet.

"So is your new boo coming to the exhibit?"

"I haven't decided yet." Jess walked over and sat on her couch.

"Jess, it's this weekend," Niecy said laughing, "Stop being scared and call that man."

Jess exhaled and rolled her eyes, "I'm not scared."

"Part of me looking up to you means I've learned how you move," Niecy said, "And Big Sis, it's giving *scared*."

Jess didn't want to admit it, but Niecy was right. Their time together was almost perfect. There was a part of her that felt apprehensive about feeling so comfortable with him. In quiet moments she felt herself wondering when that loud ass shoe would drop.

"All I'm saying is, self-sabotage is a thing and you need to stay away from it," Niecy said as if reading Jess's mind.

"You're right," Jess quietly admitted, "I'll get out of my head and invite him."

Niecy's face beamed over the video.

"Girl, go away," Jess joked, "You are *too* excited."

"I'm just happy to see you happy. I want you to stay that way. You deserve it."

Jess smiled. Niecy's words were like a warm hug she didn't know she needed.

They ended their call with "I love yous" and hung up. Jess sat with her phone in her hand. She wanted to invite Rashawn, but something was keeping her from doing it. There wasn't anything wrong, just a feeling in her gut that she shouldn't ask.

As she continued to think about it Jess realized she had gone down a rabbit hole and was officially in the land of overthinking. She wondered why she had to make things so difficult. She wondered if she was damaged after so many heartbreaks. There was nothing this man had done that should make her feel like he wasn't the man she thought he was. The problem was she didn't think her exes were capable of breaking her heart either.

Or did she and ignored the red flags? Jess shook the thoughts out of her head and found Rashawn's text thread in her phone.

Hey, she typed, attempting to keep things light.

The text bubble appeared for a moment. Disappeared. Then reappeared. Finally she saw, *Hey...hru?*

I'm good. You got plans Saturday? Jess couldn't believe that after all the time they'd spent together she felt nervous.

The typing bubble was driving Jess crazy.

Nope. Why? What's up?

*I was thinking...*Jess deleted that line...*Wanna go on a date?* She shook her head, "Delete! Why are you making things harder than they need to be?"...*Mahogany is having an exhibit and I was wondering if you were going.* Send.

Awe. Are you asking me on a date? Rashawn added a bashful emoji and Jess laughed out loud.

"I'm making too much out of this and now I got this man making fun of me," she couldn't help but laugh at herself.

Yes...now stop making fun of me. Jess added a pouting gif.

Jess laughed at herself as she watched the text bubble move on her screen. Whatever she was feeling in her gut she determined in that moment was only nerves. She had just gotten her heart broken and she didn't think she'd be ready for anything real. But it came. Sat in her face and said, "Here I am!" She couldn't continue to ignore it. She was happy.

What time would you like me to pick you up?

She smiled before her response, thinking about their first date. She'd told him about her history of heartbreak and rather than see that as a red flag, he embraced her and chose patience. Over time she'd fall in love. She just had to be open to the possibilities with Rashawn.

Jess pulled out her notebook and pen, suddenly inspired.

Thoughts are coming to me
For this piece
I'm really here delving deep into my mind to think
And consider what in the world is going on with me
You see
I'm having issues trusting what I believe to be true
I almost feel a little too blessed when I look at you

I know too blessed sounds like an oxymoron
But you reacted so beautifully when I said what's been going on
And I'm sure for me to be expressing it how I did maybe happened in the wrong forum
But I had to get the thought off my chest
Or my mind would never rest
I'm consciously removing the darkness that lived in me
So now I can see
There should never be expectations of negativity
I was in love with possibilities
Now I'm falling for reality
And I must admit it's scary
But I'm here for it - the ride
No roadblocks this time
As I try and follow the map laid out in my mind

Chapter Eighteen
Mahogany's Muse

"She thought walking away was hard to do
Until walking away led to truth
Discovering a peace that was hovering
But never before allowed to enter her soul
She thought she'd grow old and even cold
If life continued on the trajectory it was headed
Complacency seemed inevitable
Until she took a look at herself and said
"I'm betting on you"
Exploring new worlds and new views
Different energies and attitudes
Allowing her heart to be open it became consumed
By what could be described as a fantasy
Far from tragedy...no
A dream that if told in a story would seem
too good to be true
Taking the form of perfection
Physical frequencies felt through erections
Emotional energies flowing like oceans
Oshun brings forth life anew
Birthing art inspired by Mahogany's Muse."

Mahogany smiled as she saved the voice message Jess sent to her. She thought back on her trip to Jamaica. Time had flown so fast that she hadn't realized it was almost five months ago. During that vacation, she had not only found a muse, but she'd found love. One she was not sure she'd ever be able to experience again.

Tavis had tapped into a part of her that she thought was forever lost. Love wasn't at the forefront of her mind. She'd gone to Jamaica for inspiration to paint. She was a part of a well-known artistic family. Some might even say legendary.

Mahogany had stepped away from painting and focused her life on having a career as a graphic designer. It didn't take long for her to realize that her heart belonged to a paint-filled brush and a canvas. So she quit, left her fiancé', and decided to head to a beautiful island alone so she could find a muse. Tavis had been exactly that.

But they decided to leave their week of passion, romance, and love on the beach where they'd met. When she thought about him, sometimes Mahogany felt a tinge of regret. She very rarely felt that emotion but remembering his touch would send her into a longing for him. She missed Tavis so much and she wondered if a love like that could be felt twice in a lifetime.

Mahogany sat on the edge of her bed. She turned up the volume on her phone and listened to the poem Jess sent her again. Her best friend was so talented. The way she could take a week of passion and turn it into a few minutes of artistic words was unmatched.

She pressed the voice recorder button on her phone, "*Awe*, thank you, sis! I'm nervous but excited." Mahogany smiled and sent the message.

A text bubble appeared, *OTW with a pre-roll to calm ya nerves!*

Mahogany smiled again. She stood and walked to her kitchen where she opened a bottle of wine and poured it into two glasses. They planned to take a rideshare to the exhibit in a little over an hour so Jess was parking her car there. Any moment now, she would be knocking on her door. Mahogany wanted to be ready so they'd have time to laugh her nerves away.

Like clockwork, there was a knock.

"Use your key," Mahogany yelled to the door and she put the bottle in the fridge.

Jess walked in and placed her keys down, then pulled the pre-rolled blunt from her pocket and lit. Mahogany countered with a large wine glass. They looked at each other as Jess took her glass and laughed.

"Girl," Jess began, "I'm so proud of you. You've been all secretive about your work but I already know everything is going to be amazing."

"Thank you," Mahogany responded, "I want everyone to have a first time experience with this. Of course my mom has seen them, but nobody else," she paused, "I just hope everyone's first time experience is good."

"I still can't believe ya'll pulled this off in such a short time. It feels like you just got back from Jamaica yesterday," Jess said inhaling.

"Girl, I know," Mahogany sipped her wine, "My mother started planning from the moment I told her I was painting down there. That woman don't play!"

"And it doesn't hurt to have half the world following you on social media."

They laughed.

"Yeah, that too," Mahogany said, gratefully. Being a part of the Waters legacy, all eyes were on her. After a simple piece that she was only playing around with went viral, the anticipation and expectation grew immensely. She did not want to disappoint, so Jamaica was a blessing she'd always be grateful for.

Jess took a sip of her wine and looked at her friend, "You painted all of those pieces in like two months," she shook her head in disbelief, "You're already talented, we know this, but if this work shows even *half* of the passion you got from Jamaica…" she let her voice trail a moment before continuing, "I'm not expecting his face everywhere, but I know his inspiration will be and I think that's dope."

"I was locked in," Mahogany said. She thought back to the first time she noticed Tavis on the beach. She was having a bit of a block but watching him inspired her. Before she even thought about it an afternoon had gone by and a beautiful work of art was created. A piece they'd remember forever.

Mahogany paused a moment, then changed the subject, "I heard you were inviting Rashawn."

"Damn, Niecy," Jess said in the air with a laugh.

"So did you?" Mahogany said with a grin.

Jess rolled her eyes playfully, "Maybe."

"Girl, stop playing and just tell me."

Jess exhaled dramatically, "Fine," she giggled slightly, "Yeah, he's coming."

"Awe," Mahogany replied, "So wait. Why are you here instead of pullin' up lookin' like a power couple?"

"You know you're my priority today. I asked him to meet me there. He understood."

Mahogany smiled, "I'm so happy for you."

Jess smiled back.

Mahogany looked at her friend's glowing smile and her heart filled. Jess had gone through her share of heartbreak and the confusion finding new love often brings. The stars had seemed to finally align and her frequency tuned into his and they just brought about an energy that could be seen a million galaxies away. There was a peace that words could never truly express.

A work of art began to come to life in her mind. That type of love didn't come often, but when it did…wow. She would know. She'd felt it only months before. No amount of time spent in previous relationships compared to what she experienced on the beaches of Jamaica.

Thoughts of Tavis filled Mahogany's mind once again. She couldn't shake him. Knowing her words held power, she spoke.

"I miss him, and I won't lie, I wish he were here."

"Awe, friend," Jess touched Mahogany's hand, "It's ok to miss him."

"Sometimes I wish we had exchanged numbers or something," Mahogany paused in thought.

Jess sighed, "It would've been too much. Everything was still so fresh with his situation. Ya'll needed a moment."

"But now that moment may be forever."

"Life can be funny," Jess said, "When two people are drawn together by their souls the most unlikely sequence of events will happen to bring them together."

Jess's words felt like a warm hug that pulled Mahogany in. Her best friend, sister, always knew what to say and, more importantly, exactly when to say it. That's what she needed to hear. Though she made her decision to walk away with a logical mind, her heart had begun to take over completely.

She couldn't imagine another man coming into her life and having the effect Tavis had on her. He calmed her spirit. Their heartbeats matched when they lay next to each other. She felt safe with him.

"Our car is about to pull up," Jess said.

"Ok," Mahogany replied, snapping back to the moment. This very important moment.

"You ready?"

Mahogany exhaled deeply and shook the tension from her shoulders. She smiled and looked at Jess.

"Let me go shut this city down real quick."

"Oooh, okaaaay!" Jess co-signed.

Tavis would have to be another thought for another day. It was time to think of him only as the muse that inspired the work she was displaying this very evening. Love of art would be the focus, her being stuck in love would be tomorrow's worries. Tonight, was the time to display Mahogany's muse.

Chapter Nineteen
The Other Side Of Insanity

Jess smiled broadly as she took in the scene. The gallery was comfortably packed. Champagne glasses remained full as guests admired the beautiful artwork that encompassed the room. What she'd seen before was almost nothing compared to the finished pieces Mahogany had chosen for the exhibit. She could clearly imagine the beaches of Jamaica, the sounds of children, and the fiery love that had enflamed her best friend's heart.

"I knew Mahogany was dope, I mean she's a Waters, but damn," Rashawn said walking up behind Jess.

He handed her a glass of champagne and touched the small of her back. She felt a gentle shiver with his touch as she inhaled him. Lawd, he smelled so good.

"Yeah, she showed out with this," Jess replied.

"Who's the guy," Rashawn asked, pointing to the face that filled the canvas in front of them.

"Her muse," she responded with a laugh, "His name is Tavis. She met him while she was down in Jamaica."

"Looks like she fell in love."

"You can see that?"

"Anyone can if they look," he smiled and walked closer to the piece. He turned toward the bar with a look of recognition.

Mahogany turned and her breath caught in her throat.

"That's him right there, right?" Rashawn asked, nodding his head in the direction of the man at the bar.

It was him. Tavis. How?

"I'll be right back," she said as she handed her glass to Rashawn.

It only took a moment to find Mahogany and exchange a conversation through a set of stares.

Jess: Girl!

Mahogany: Girrrl!

Jess: Meet me in the bathroom!

Mahogany: Give me a sec.

Jess nodded her understanding to her friend and headed toward the restrooms. Mahogany entered shortly after she did.

"What is he doing here?" Mahogany asked as she entered.

"So you saw him?"

"Yes, girl!" Mahogany rolled her eyes.

"I thought you wanted to see him," Jess responded, confused.

Mahogany stopped and stared for a moment.

"Wait," Jess said, "who are you talking about?"

"Who are *you* talking about?" Mahogany responded.

"Tavis," Jess said, "Rashawn just saw him at the bar."

Mahogany's eyes widened and a huge smile filled her face.

"Are you serious?"

"Yes," Jess said, "but who were you talking about?"

Mahogany's smile faded, "Erick," she paused a moment, "And he has flowers too."

Jess rolled her eyes and annoyance consumed her.

"When we were together he was living the single life. I let him go and now he won't leave me alone."

"I get it Jess, but please take it outside. I can't have him acting up in here like he did at Niecy's birthday," Mahogany said.

Jess nodded her head as Mahogany turned to the mirror. She shook off her annoyance. Erick would be dealt with, but right now something really special was happening with her friend and she needed to be there for her.

"He looks better than the picture, girl," Jess said.

Mahogany smiled, "I can't believe he's here. Like, how?"

"I told you that hearts that are meant to be together will find their way, come whatever."

"Hush yo' poetic ass up before you make me cry and mess up my makeup," Mahogany said with a smile.

They walked out together and quickly separated to head toward their targets.

Tavis looked better than Mahogany remembered. He seemed more...perfect. As if feeling her presence he turned from the painting of the beach where they'd met and smiled. They locked eyes and the room emptied, much like their first dance in that little bar on the beach of Jamaica.

They walked toward each other and Mahogany felt like she was in one of those old romance movies.

"Hello," Tavis said with the smile she'd fallen in love with. He embraced her and they could feel their hearts fall into rhythm.

Mahogany's heart quickened, "How?"

"You're not hard to find," he laughed as he reluctantly pulled away.

"But what about-"

His eyes saddened. The way it did with deep loss.

"I'm sorry," she said softly.

"I know we said we left it on the island but I couldn't stop thinking about you," he said, redirecting the conversation back to its purpose.

"I'm glad you did," Mahogany smiled, "I've been thinking about you too."

Mahogany's heart felt full. This night couldn't be more perfect. The exhibit was a complete success. When Jess caught her attention she had just learned that all of her pieces had been sold. And to top it off the man who had taken her heart and filled it was now standing in front of her with love in his eyes.

Jess watched on as she witnessed a love that had grown stronger with time and distance. Anyone could see they were meant to be. She only hoped they'd recognize what they clearly have and move forward.

Meanwhile, dealing with Erick was nothing short of insanity. He was everything she wanted to avoid in love, while Rashawn seemed to be everything she had prayed for. Tonight she knew she was on the other side of insanity. It felt amazing to get through it. She couldn't ask for more.

I'm on the other side of insanity
I feel peace
No more thoughts of you consuming me
I'm finally in love with me
I tried to rely on my heart
But my mind was confined to the dark
Now I'm on the other side

No more questions of why
No more what ifs
Cuz "If" has never been able to live within
On the other side of insanity
Lives a sane reality
Figments of dreams only grow
If you know which can be
So on this side
I'm alive, new life
New vibe
New energy
On the other side of insanity

Chapter Twenty
When Petty Goes Wrong

"Hey Mahogany," Rashawn said, interrupting what seemed to be a deep conversation.

"Hey Rashawn," Mahogany said with a smile, "This is Tavis. My muse."

Rashawn and Tavis greeted each other.

"Have you seen Jess?"

Did Mahogany's eyes widened for a split second or was he imagining things?

"I'm not sure. She's around here somewhere."

Rashawn thanked Mahogany, acknowledged Tavis once again, and walked away. Where had Jess gone? He understood now why she had left so abruptly when she'd spotted the man at the bar. But after giving Mahogany the heads up why hadn't she come back to him?

"Hey Niecy," he said.

Niecy turned around and smiled, "Hey!"

"Have you seen Jess?" Rashawn said, attempting to sound nonchalant. He felt like he was failing miserably.

"Awe, look at you missin' yo' bae," she giggled.

He could see her buzz from the alcohol in her eyes.

"You good?" He asked.

"Yup," she replied, "Jess is over there," she pointed toward the door, "Well she *was*."

He never considered himself a man who needed to know where his lady was at all times, but he still had a gut feeling something was up. As he scanned the room he still didn't see her. Maybe she was outside smoking some weed just taking it all in.

As he stepped outside, his heart sank. There she was. With her ex. The same one that had caused a scene at the bar. Erick, right? He could see the smile on her face as she took the bouquet and they hugged. He could see her say something and turn to walk away. Erick followed.

Turning on his heels, Rashawn's heart sank further. He wouldn't allow it to show on his face, but he was hurting and disappointed. As he walked back inside the gallery he placed the glasses of champagne, one for him and a refill for Jess, on a small table in a corner and walked out.

*****

"I accept your apology," Jess said as she turned to walk away. She noticed Erick following and stopped.

"Where are you going?"

"It would be pretty selfish of me to walk into Mahogany's event with a bouquet for myself," she said with a slight laugh, "Do you have any cash?"

"Cash?" Erick said while reaching into his pocket and pulling out a bill.

"Good. A twenty."

Jess took the bill and walked to the corner to a lady she'd noticed as they first walked outside. She had a small child, maybe 5 or 6, with her as she held a sign asking for help.

"Hey sweetheart," she said to the little girl, "You are so beautiful just like these flowers."

The little girl smiled.

"I think you should have them."

The little girl looked at her mother and smiled again when she received her approval.

"Thank you," the little girl said.

"You're most welcome," Jess replied. She looked at the lady and placed the money in her hand.

"Thank you," she said.

"You're welcome, Queen," Jess replied.

She turned to see Erick staring at her with a lost look in his eyes. She touched his elbow as she walked passed and he turned to follow.

When Erick approached her, Jess felt pure frustration and aggravation. She wondered what would make him pop up here. It had been some time since they'd last spoken . She'd blocked him on everything even before the bar incident. Her closure from him was complete, but she couldn't lie, accountability from this man was icing on the cake.

He'd explained that he wasn't proud of how things ended and his behavior afterward. He was in a selfish place. He finally admitted his other relationship and confessed that Jess was a rebound. It stung to hear it, but she got a bit of pleasure to learn that Tia had left him alone too. That was the reason for the incident at the bar. He was hurt because he went from having his cake and eating it too, to having an empty plate.

Jess had no desire to hold a grudge forever. Her life was about peace. Mama Copeland had taught her that her peace is the center of everything. Without it she could not think clearly or love fully. Forgiving Erick had confirmed in her mind that she was over it and him. She could move on freely with Rashawn.

Rashawn! Dammit! She'd been so caught up in her conversation with Erick that she hadn't realized how much time had passed. She had rushed Erick outside so quickly so as not to make a scene.

"I really do appreciate the apology and the flowers," she said as they reached the door, "I hope you find whatever it is you're looking for."

"Damn, Jess," Erick said with clear hurt in his voice.

"Erick, we're good," she said with a soft smile, "I just have something really good happening in my life. I need to get back to him."

With that, she turned on her heel and walked inside.

"Jess," she heard Mahogany call as she walked toward her.

"Have you seen Rashawn?"

"Sweetheart, he left."

Jess looked around but didn't see him, "Why did he leave without saying anything?"

Mahogany exhaled, "I'm guessing he saw you with Erick. He came looking for you then I saw him walk outside and come right back in, then he just...left."

Jess felt the deep frown that crossed her face. How could she have messed up so badly? She should've just asked Mahogany to have him escorted out. She didn't need his apology. She was happy now that he was out of her life.

If she were to be honest with herself she'd have to admit she only spoke to Erick because of her petty pride. Jess wasn't a fool. She knew he was up to something when he arrived with flowers. She wanted to be able to say she'd moved on. She wanted to make a fool of him.

Instead, she made a fool of herself. Rashawn had left with no words. He saw what he saw and she had to admit that if she were on the other side and had no real context she'd likely see the same. The only question she had left to ask was how she would fix it.

Jess wanted to believe that a simple conversation would mend it all, but how could she be sure? She could tell he cared about her deeply and she knew she was slowly falling for him. With their bond she knew he had to be hurt.

"Why did I even entertain him?" Jess asked no one in particular.

"Do you want to go see if you can catch him?" Mahogany asked.

Jess shook her head back and forth, "I don't even know what to say right now."

"Well, we're about to wrap it all up. You want to stay at my spot tonight?"

Jess looked up and saw Tavis headed toward them, "Damn, sis, I forgot about Tavis. Don't worry about me. I'll be fine. I'll burn some sage and call him tomorrow," she smiled as Tavis approached, "Your muse is here. One of us needs to have a perfect evening and this is clearly your night."

Mahogany hugged Jess before she introduced Tavis. Jess made small conversations as her mind drifted...

> *It looks like being petty*
> *might've just gotten the best of me*
> *My need to make him receive my last word*
> *Has now placed me in an absurd position*
> *I should've listened when my conscience*
> *Told me to stay conscious of my surroundings*

But something overwhelming
Came over, well, ME
And it's like I couldn't control my petty
So now I'm standing alone
With my phone in hand
Wondering if I really just lost my man
Over some petty get back
As I look at my best friend and see her heart filled
I realize I just might've lost that
That once in a lifetime
That oooh girl he's all mine
All because I couldn't just leave the past behind
Now I'm
Not sure if it's pain or pride
But there is a battle between heart and mind
My heart wanting to text him and make it all right
On the other side, it's like out of mind out of sight
...Or whatever they said...
Instead of choosing him I'm choosing
to keep me protected
From heartbreak and unwanted lessons
I know I might be running but
When it comes to love I have zero luck
I know petty is not a virtue
And now I'm stuck confused
So how do I continue?
I wanted a perfect love song
But it seems this is what happens when
petty goes wrong

Chapter Twenty-One
Unwritten

Jess took a seat at the table across from Mahogany in the café they'd decided to meet in.

"I ordered a green tea for you," Mahogany said gesturing toward the mug in front of her.

"Thank you, girl, I need it," Jess placed her bag next to her in an empty chair that sat to the side of them, "You're glowing."

Mahogany smiled wide, "Girl," she grinned, "I still can't believe he came."

"I'm so happy for you. This is real love," Jess said.

"Last night was amazing," Mahogany said through a memory, "It might have been better than before. I don't know. It felt more..." she paused in thought, "permanent."

"Awe. You really deserve it."

"You deserve it too you know," Mahogany said softly as she sipped her tea.

Jess shifted uncomfortably.

"Did you reach out to him yet?" Mahogany said.

Jess shifted in her seat again and shook her head "no" as she took a sip of her tea.

Mahogany rolled her eyes, "Why not?"

The ladies sat wordless as the sounds of the café filled their silence.

"This is a real simple fix, you know," Mahogany said gently.

Jess sighed, "When I got back home I started thinking. Why didn't he just say something? Even text and curse me out. He just," she paused, "left."

Mahogany wanted to approach her answer gently because she had been in this place before. The place of falling into fear because love seems like too much.

"Yeah, I get it," said Mahogany, "but I think you're trying to find a way out of this because you're scared."

The reality struck Jess in her stomach.

"Look, I'm not saying you can't wonder those things," Mahogany continued, "But I *am* saying when you weigh it all out is it worth it to let him walk away like that? I think you'd regret it."

"I promised myself that if I started to feel doubts I would stop and think. I've let my gut feeling be ignored too many times and I just get hurt in the end," Jess responded.

"Mama Copeland once told me that when we've been hurt and we're scared to take down that wall we name our hurt and our fear 'intuition'," Mahogany said using air quotes.

Jess sighed. Her mother had said those words to her a few times as well. When they were speaking about other people it was easy to understand, but now that she had the mirror facing herself it was a hard pill to swallow.

"Don't self-sabotage," Mahogany said.

"Is that what I'm doing?" Jess felt defeated, "Why am I so afraid?"

"Because you've been through a lot," Mahogany answered, "We both have. You think I'm not scared out of my mind right now? It was easy and comfortable when I thought it was a spring fling type of situation, but now he's here."

Jess smiled as she watched Mahogany's face brighten without effort.

Mahogany continued, "I tell you what though. I refuse to let this love go without even trying. It feels too good," she looked Jess deeply in her eyes, "I can see your aura and it is all so beautiful since Rashawn. Brighter than I've ever seen before. Don't use this pothole as an entire roadblock to your happiness."

Jess sat in silence. She knew every word her friend said was true. She could've called Rashawn that night and told him about the conversation that took place with Erick. She could have apologized for the confusion. Everything in her told her that he would understand.

Everything had flowed so easily between them that fear had no space to truly enter, but as soon as an excuse presented itself she was ready to jump all over it. She knew for sure that she was completely over Erick. Time had passed and he was out of sight and out of mind. When he did show up she believed she handled it well.

It was time for her to put her big girl panties on and fix this before it went too far.

Both of their phones rang simultaneously, interrupting their silence. They looked at their screens.

"I'll answer," Mahogany said, looking at Niecy's group video call.

"Hey beautiful," Jess said moving her chair closer to Mahogany to share the screen.

"Hey, ya'll," Niecy replied, "First of all, Mahogany, last night was so lit."

"I can tell," Mahogany said, laughing, "I saw you enjoyed the champagne."

"And the men," Niecy added.

"Yeah, you did have some fine, eligible bachelors there," Jess said.

"Speaking of fine," Niecy said, "I saw your man and he was looking for you."

"Oh, he found me," Jess responded with a sigh.

"Wait," Niecy paused in thought, "Awe man, did I see Erick there last night or am I trippin'?"

"Nah, you're not trippin'," Mahogany answered.

"Please don't tell me-" Niecy started.

Jess interrupted, "Then don't ask because exactly what you think happened, happened."

Niecy's mouth dropped, "Well tell me you weren't out there tongue wrestling with that loud, rude ass man-child."

"Damn," Mahogany said in response to Niecy's description of Erick.

"Nah, nothing like that. I think he may have come out at a bad time though." Jess went on to explain the events that took place from the apology to the homeless mother and daughter she'd given his flowers and money.

Niecy stared at the screen as she heard the details. When Jess was finished she shook her head and grinned.

"What?" Jess asked.

"You are cold a.f."

Mahogany let a laugh slip. Jess turned to her in playful disbelief.

"I didn't mean to be cold," Jess said, "But I needed him to understand that flowers and an apology are cool, but they don't fix anything."

"Well I'm sorry for telling him where you were," Niecy said, "I had no idea."

"It's not on you," Jess replied.

Mahogany shook her head, "Not on you at all. But now we have Jess over here self-sabotaging."

Niecy rolled her eyes, "Oh lawd. What's up with that?"

"She won't call this man to explain. She's trying to make it into an intuition thing."

"Well Mama Copeland told me once that sometimes we call our fear intuition."

Mahogany laughed and Jess shook her head with a grin.

"That seems to be the theme, huh?" Jess said.

Mahogany chimed in, "I literally just told her the same thing."

"So you know there has to be some truth to it," Niecy said.

"Fine, ya'll," Jess said, "I'll call him."

"Good," Mahogany said, "So on to you. How's Arizona?"

"Beautiful, as usual. I wish I could bottle the views and bring them home, but leave the heat," Niecy's eyes opened wider, "Guys, it is a hundred and hell out here."

The ladies laughed in unison.

"So are you ready to see your dad?" Jess asked.

"I'm so beyond ready. Time just seemed to slow down as soon as I got on the plane," Niecy paused and tears began to fill her eyes, "Ya'll I'm so grateful. Thank you for doing this. I'll never be able to say how much this means for real, for real."

Jess smiled, "Awe, you're welcome, love. You both deserve a fresh start."

"Make sure when you see him you give him an extra hug from all of us," Mahogany said, "One less black man in this jacked up system. It's a time to celebrate."

"Most definitely," Jess responded.

They talked for a few more moments about the release of Niecy's father. Her excitement, her plans, even her concerns about him adjusting once he was home. They laughed and comforted each other with positive affirmations. Then they ended the call with a promise to reach out once he was with Niecy.

As if on cue, Jess's mind shifted right back to the intrusive memory of the night before. They were right. She'd made a mountain out of a molehill and the more time she took to address it the worse it would get.

The last thing she needed was to let a good thing go because of her own fears. She'd closed past chapters and was ready to end that entire book of her life. She wanted a clean slate to begin a new story. One that presently was unwritten but had the potential to be the greatest story she'd ever told.

I...am...petrified
I was completely caught off guard, absolutely surprised
When you said you had a true interest in you and I
And I damn near lost my mind when you looked
into my eyes
On that one chaotic night
You remember, right?
I know you do
Because in that moment I knew you felt it too
But due to my past I allowed myself to feel confused
Trying to navigate my emotions because I was
falling for you
I was concerned that maybe it was too soon
But what is time when concerning the hearts of two
That's why I gotta say fuck it
Take the chance and jump off the cliff
Blindly in love with no parachute
Cuz I'm betting on you
Yeah, I'm betting on black
I'm talking love to be exact
Melanated magic mixed with the mystery
Of where we will be
Moments from now, days from now, years from now
Our energies screaming so loud
That this is what it's all about
At that point I will sit and recount
The steps it took to get there
Step one was relinquishing all fear
The next step being this moment when I must confess
I was trippin' and I have no excuses
I allowed you to believe what you see
Providing no clarity
Afraid that if you knew the truth
You'd want to pursue
And I'd be left with my heart out there fragile

Vulnerable as I trust it with you
But I have to
When I look ahead into happiness all I see is you
You inspire my pen to fill blank pages
With hope of bringing truth to my imaginations
You are my muse for
My lyrics to an unwritten future

Chapter Twenty-Two
Share My Life With...

Rashawn picked up his phone and found Jess's number. He began to touch the screen when he stopped. If he were to be honest with himself he had to admit that while it was frustration mixed with hurt that caused him to walk out of the gallery without a word to Jess, it was pride that kept him from calling her now.

He'd already dealt with relationships where he chased, but he was tired of feeling like a predator chasing prey. He'd learned early that women are intentional with how they deal with men. If they want you they let you know in one way or another.

Talking to a recent ex-boyfriend outside of the gallery where she was on a date was not something that happened by accident. Jess had to know what she was doing. Rashawn had observed a long time ago that she was an educated and sensible woman. He refused to insult her intelligence by pretending like she was some oblivious woman with no idea of how her actions could affect him.

Walking away was hard. It was quite embarrassing as well, truth be told. He remembered feeling like everyone in the room was staring at him as he turned from the glass doors that led outside to where he witnessed Erick giving Jess flowers and her accepting them with a smile and a hug.

Even when she turned to walk away, it wasn't to come back inside. No, she was walking away from the building. Erick followed as she led. Rashawn couldn't bear to witness anything else.

It had been years since he'd felt the way he did with Jess. As a matter of fact, he could argue he'd never quite felt this way about anyone before. She was different. Everything flowed between them. From their small talk at Verse One to her moments of silent comfort on the night of their run in with the police. She seemed to know what to do without even trying.

So how did she miss this? He'd left without saying anything because he didn't want to talk right then. Mahogany had worked hard for that moment and he didn't want to ruin it with what had the potential to be a hurt filled conversation. Their first disagreement didn't need to be in the middle of an art exhibit.

But it had been two days and he hadn't heard a word. This wasn't the first time he'd picked up the phone to call. He'd even considered just stopping by, but his mother taught him a long time ago to never just show up at the home of someone he'd just started dating. If there hadn't been a formal commitment there was freedom to do as one pleased so unless he wanted to find out who else was in the running for her heart, he needed to respect boundaries.

So, what was left to do? He didn't want things to end with no explanation, but Rashawn believed he was owed the call. If she was running away, he would not chase after her.

The buzz of the phone still in his hand startled Rashawn from his thought.

Hey. Can we talk tonight after Verse One?

His heart pounded in his ear as he read Jess's text message. He'd hoped to see her that night and at least gauge her energy, but a part of him thought she might avoid going at all. A tiny smile crept in the corner of his lips before he cleared his throat and wiped it away.

Yeah, that's koo.

He responded. He waited and watched the notification go from *Delivered* to *Read*, but no text bubbled appeared after.

Rashawn placed his phone down on the table in front of him and sat back. Overthinking was not something he was used to doing and he had no intentions of starting in that moment.

He did what always came naturally to him in a moment of cloudiness in his mind. His outlet. His therapy.

He picked up his old beat up notebook that held pages and pages of scattered thoughts and found a clean page somewhere randomly in the middle. He pulled the pen from the metal spiral that held it all together and began to transform his thoughts into rhyme.

Man...I thought I found my rib
But just like that she became the sensation of
another man's fingertip
Was I stupid
To allow this woman to enter
Making her the center of my thoughts
I thought that she would be my future
I believed in the power of me and her

*I dug deep and retrieved my heart from a hidden place
A space set aside for the one I'd share my life with...*

*****

Jess stared at her phone as she re-read Rashawn's response.

Yeah, that's koo.

How was she supposed to read that? She found text messages annoying in moments like this. Mama Copeland once told her that when people read other's messages the reader interprets the tone based on their own state of mind, which could lead to miscommunications and confusion.

In her mind she heard an attitude of nonchalance. That tone could mean he didn't care or he was over the whole situation. Jess had known that Rashawn was not someone who enjoyed drama of any kind. He kept things cool and beyond having to cut someone drunk and belligerent off once in a while, she'd never seen him really flip out on anyone. Even when they were pulled over the first night she'd gone to his home he still kept it pretty cool.

She couldn't help but think that her need to be petty toward Erick had hurt her chances with Rashawn. Was it really worth it to get the last laugh? Hell, could she even consider it the last laugh if she walked away losing her potential soul mate?

Jess thought back to the night when they'd heard that artist speak on Soul Ties. They both knew that even though the artist didn't have a clue, she was speaking directly to them. Their souls had tied before they'd even touched. Their frequencies were aligned and their energy intertwined. Their intimacy had only strengthened the bond.

But now it was all at risk because she just *had* to get her lick back. She just *had* to make Erick feel as humiliated as she'd felt when she received that call from his ex. It was like she couldn't help herself at that moment. But now looking back she didn't have to wonder, she knew it wasn't worth it.

Getting over Rashawn, as short-lived as it may have been, would be the hardest thing she'd ever have to do. Seven days wouldn't be enough. She could feel it.

Jess's heart sank as she put down her phone. She'd been staring for minutes before she accepted that there was no further response she'd receive. That one line was it:

Yeah, that's koo.

Jess jumped as her phone alerted her to an incoming call. She grabbed it quickly and sighed as she saw *Mama* on the screen.

"Hey Mama," Jess said.

"Hey, baby," Mama Copeland said softly, "How are you feeling this morning?"

"Not too good."

"What's going on?"

"I think I messed things up with Rashawn and I know you're probably going to say I jumped into it too quickly, but Mama, you don't understand, he's different," Jess rambled.

Mama Copeland took a beat to allow Jess's words to settle before she spoke. She knew her daughter so she understood her need to get her thoughts out. Jess wouldn't be open to hearing until her own thoughts were emptied into the atmosphere.

"Has he said you messed things up?"

"No," Jess almost whispered.

"Then how do you know you messed things up?"

Jess sat in silence. Mama Copeland allowed her the moment. Finally Jess broke down and told her mother everything. Her deep feelings for Rashawn, her pettiness toward Erick, and how her pride kept her from confronting the situation head on.

"I know you had to leave early,, but I wish you could've been there mama," Jess said, "You would've stopped me from-"

"I would not have done any such thing," Mama Copeland interrupted, "You are an adult and I can advise, but I will not stop you from doing what you want to do. I raised you, baby girl, and I believe I've done a fantastic job. It's up to you whether or not you make me a liar."

Jess took in the words of her mother. She knew better and Mama Copeland was the last person to allow her to live in a made up world of oblivion.

"Do you want to fix it?"

Jess's response was quick, "Yes."

"Then you know what you need to do. Damn this whole pride thing. If you want your man back then you need to swallow all of that and make it right."

One of her favorite things about her mother was that she always gave the facts to her straight, no chaser. One of her mother's favorite sayings was, "If you have a problem you have two choices. You either fix it or learn from it. Either way worrying is not a factor because it changes nothing." She did not believe in sitting around complaining about a situation that could be resolved.

"You always know when to call and what to say when you do," Jess said softly.

"I'm your mama. We are forever connected," was her simple reply.

"I love you, mama."

"I love you back."

There was nothing like a mother's love. Mama Copeland could heal her with words like no other person on this earth could.

With him I thought I'd have it all
Even though I thought it was too early to fall
My heart took a nosedive anyway
And I'd never want to hurt him in any way
But I allowed my revenge to get the best of me
Now I'm alone wondering how this could be?
Have I lost the keeper of my rib?

My soul's inhabitant
The dweller of my heart that I thought I'd share
my life with...

Chapter Twenty-Three
I'm Sorry

Jess could feel the pounding in her chest as she walked into Verse One. Her heart felt a pull toward him before their eyes met. She couldn't help but stare as Rashawn finished mixing a drink and handed it to a patron.

Rashawn felt Jess's presence as he took the payment for the drink he'd just served. He wanted to ignore the urge to look and allow her to approach him. After all, she'd reached out to him. However, his heart had a mind of its own and it seemed his eyes were in cahoots.

He turned and their eyes locked. So much emotion in one glance. She could feel his pain and he could feel her guilt. Rashawn chose to simply nod an acknowledgment of her presence before responding to the call of another patron in need of a drink.

Jess had no idea how to receive that cordial recognition so she just returned a half smile and walked to an open seat. She knew what she was about to do was a little corny, but it was the only way she knew how to express her exact feelings and thoughts without risking a miscommunication of the stumbling words that would fall tragically from her lips. As strong and intelligent as she knew herself to be, Jess could easily find herself dumb as she searched for the appropriate words. So this had to be it.

Rashawn watched Jess walk to a seat and sit down. The way she caught the attention of everyone she passed, greeting each of them as if they were the most important person in the room, only displayed the beautiful energy that engulfed her.

"How ya'll doing tonight?"

Jess switched her attention to the host of the evening. Rashawn did the same.

"We got any newcomers this evening?" The crowd responded with a few waves and exclamations, "My name is Khani and I'm your host for the evening."

Khani continued with his introductions, allowing the crown to warm up for the evening.

Jess shifted in her seat. She hadn't been nervous to recite a piece in years. Her stomach turned in knots as she took deep breaths to release the anxiety. Her head cleared a bit as she heard Khani invite her on stage.

Rashawn paused and stared at Jess as she made her way to the mic.

"Now usually I don't do this but uuuuh..." Jess said pulling her phone out and touching the screen, "I just wrote this and there is a need to do it here, tonight."

She knew she had to play it all cool so as not to reveal her raw emotions. The crowd responded with "Talk yo' shit" and "Get 'em sis" and "Speak Queen". Jess felt a sense of peace as she received the reassuring vibes.

"The first time I say I love you

I want it to be beautiful
Clear comprehension of not just a love,
but that I am IN love with you
But I caused confusion
When I felt the need to establish a conclusion
To an illusion I foolishly thought was love
Allowed my ego to lead me
Not thinking of how I selfishly only considered
what would feel good to me
But it was only a temporary satisfaction
A distraction from the real problem
I've got baggage, a lot of them
And I've built a wall hard to tumble
And so I wonder if somehow now I fumbled the ball
I was even scared to call
Afraid you'd turn me away if I came to your door
So I ignored the passing time hoping
it would just go away
Like if I called you'd tell me you don't want to stay
On this path we've begun?
What we have glows more vivid than the moon
and shines more radiant than the sun
But I fear we're done
I don't want to believe it though
So I've decided to step in front of a mic at a show
To show you I'm serious
I'm in this
No more games no more questions
Just let me know I'm not too late
But even if I am I want you to know that I now
and forever will love you anyway
I'm sorry"

Rashawn felt his heart rate accelerate. He watched Jess as she made her way back to her seat. She picked up her bag and headed toward him.

"Can you take a break?" Jess asked as she approached the bar.

Rashawn nodded and motioned for the other bartender that he was stepping away.

Jess led him to the patio that was now empty as the crowd took in the next artist on stage. The woman graced the audience with a smooth song about her love for her soulmate. The moment was not missed by either of them.

Rashawn intentionally kept an even expression. A poem, as dope as it was, could not be how they resolved this issue. He knew without accountability this stumbling block could grow into an entire wall between them if not handled correctly. On both sides.

"What's up?" Rashawn said as they stepped outside.

Jess had imagined this conversation all day. She envisioned finishing the poem she wrote for him and not having to say a word. She'd hoped she wouldn't have to say much at all. That he'd tell her he felt the same and all of the misunderstandings and miscommunications would be of the past and they could move forward as if nothing ever happened.

But it was clear that wouldn't work. He wanted a conversation and it was obvious.

"I'm sorry," Jess said, "I was being petty. Wanting to get my lick back on my ex for the headache he gave me and I didn't regard your feelings at all."

"Do you still care about him?" The question was flat and it caught Jess off guard a bit.

"Not at all," she responded.

"Enough to disregard me, though."

The words stung and it left her speechless.

"But I was wrong too," he said looking into her eyes.

Jess returned his gaze but with a question in her eyes.

Rashawn continued, "My wall was up a little too, so I made an assumption and didn't allow you to clear all this up."

"I don't blame you," Jess said, "I can see now how it looked."

They stood in silence. Both contemplating their next words. Jess had never been with a man that she could be vulnerable with the way she found herself with Rashawn. And when she showed that side he'd surprised her and taken responsibility for our disconnect. Something he didn't need to do because she'd created the situation, he had only reacted. But he did. And it meant the world to her.

Rashawn replayed his apology in his mind and in the moment realized that his heart was hers. She had taken it, nurtured it, and even when she cracked it a bit she hadn't broken it. Instead she came back humbly and mended it. He was used to women who never thought they were wrong and always had an excuse for every bad act, but she was different. So when she held herself accountable he had no choice but to do the same.

Rashawn put his arm around Jess's waist and pulled her close. He hugged her tightly, both feeling their hearts had not fallen out of sync. He pulled back slightly and she looked up into his eyes.

Their heart pounded together.

"I love you too," he said softly in her ear.

Jess's heart raced, and she felt his keep pace. Rashawn leaned down as she tilted her head back, accepting the sweet kiss he offered her lips. The song that played in their background ended and they pulled apart.

Their souls were tied. The past had started where their present left them. As their heartbeats slowed down together into a comfortable rhythm they looked forward to their future. The prologue to their novel of love was already complete. They knew within their hearts that this moment marked the start of their true story. The future held blank pages and their souls were the pens to fill them with a beautiful story of love still unwritten.

Made in the USA
Columbia, SC
28 May 2024